"FIRE AGAIN," CAPTAIN JAMES T. KIRK COMMANDED . . .

. . . raising his voice. "Hold for two minutes this time." Again the beam lashed the alien, and again it winked out, leaving no sign of an opening, no sign of damage. If full power from the ship's phasers was having so little effect, then photon torpedoes might not do any better. The alien would not be easily destroyed.

As Spock's voice broke the silence that followed, it seemed to Kirk that the first officer's baritone almost echoed through the corridors of the alien vessel. "You must fire photon torpedoes within the next hour to have any hope of diverting the object's course . . . or of destroying it in time."

The Vulcan might be pronouncing his own death sentence. . . .

STAR TREK®

HEART OF THE SUN

PAMELA SARGENT
and GEORGE ZEBROWSKI

POCKET BOOKS

New York   London   Toronto   Sydney   Tokyo   Singapore

This book is a work of fiction. Names, characters, places and incidents are products of the authors' imagination or are used fictitiously. Any resemblance to actual events or locales or persons, living or dead, is entirely coincidental.

An *Original* Publication of POCKET BOOKS

 POCKET BOOKS, a division of Simon & Schuster Inc. 1230 Avenue of the Americas, New York, NY 10020

This book is published by Pocket Books, a division of Simon & Schuster Inc., under exclusive license from Paramount Pictures.

All rights reserved, including the right to reproduce this book or portions thereof in any form whatsoever. For information address Pocket Books, 1230 Avenue of the Americas, New York, NY 10020

ISBN: 0-671-00237-6

First Pocket Books printing November 1997

10 9 8 7 6 5 4 3 2 1

POCKET and colophon are registered trademarks of Simon & Schuster Inc.

Printed in the U.S.A.

To our friend, Ted Brock,
who learned from everyone
but always knew how to watch *Star Trek*

We may choose something like a star
To stay our minds on and be staid.

—Robert Frost

HEART OF THE SUN

Chapter One

"RIGHT HERE—" Commander Spock said as he pointed to the flashing dot on the sector display, "—in the cometary ring of this solar system, there is an object that does not belong."

He paused, as if for dramatic effect, though Kirk knew that his science officer was above such gestures. Spock continued. "It is clearly artificial, Captain, a fact confirmed by its heat signature, which is increasing too precisely for a natural source."

"Could it be Romulan?" Kirk asked. They were close enough to the Neutral Zone between Federation space and the Romulan Empire for that to be possible.

"Unlikely, Captain. Our first indications were that it was a planetary body that had long been part of the ring. Our records show it has been there for some time. There is no evidence to suggest the Romulans would have intruded so far into this sector."

Kirk looked at his friend, and for a moment shared with him the rush of discovery that was curiosity's reward. But the moment passed, and he said, "Unfortunately, we can't even think of investigating that object until after we complete our mission on Tyrtaeus II."

"Understood," Spock replied, peering at the display, and for an instant, James Kirk remembered when he had once thought that he would never really know the Vulcan as he knew Leonard McCoy, Montgomery Scott, Uhura, or the other members of his crew. Once, he had believed that Spock would always be a stranger, as he was to most human beings. Kirk had wondered if the distance between them might widen into a gulf.

But he had learned to see through Spock's inscrutability, just as he could gaze into Lieutenant Uhura's dark eyes and see if some private, unspoken concern was worrying her, and know from the cheerful, enthusiastic look on Hikaru Sulu's face that the helmsman was about to launch into a discussion of his latest hobby. Spock's raising of his eyebrow when confronted with yet another example of human foolishness betrayed not only his wonderment at human irrationality, but also his amusement at such illogical behavior. Spock had a good sense of humor—for a Vulcan, Kirk mused. Of course, his stoic friend would never acknowledge that openly.

The composed but intent expression on Spock's face now told Kirk that his science officer was extremely curious about the unknown object on the display.

"Investigating that object," Kirk said as he gestured at the sensor display screen above Spock's computer, "would be a lot more interesting than this mission's likely to be. At least we'll have something to look forward to after we're done on Tyrtaeus II, right, Spock?"

Spock was silent. Kirk suppressed a grin. The Vulcan would sooner die than admit how eager he was to get the diplomacy out of the way, so that the crew could move onto what they did best: exploring the unknown.

Occasionally Kirk could grasp his comrade's unspoken thoughts only as one would observe icebergs floating down from their calving waters in Earth's polar regions, seeing only the small portion that showed above the surface while sensing the leviathan hidden below.

"I'm picking up a message from Tyrtaeus II," Lieutenant Uhura said, interrupting Kirk's reflections. "It's exactly the same as the one we picked up earlier." She frowned, then recited the message. "'We look forward to restoration of our data base soon—Myra Coles.'"

No salutation, Kirk thought, no niceties of expression, no hint that the Tyrtaeans might be grateful for any aid the crew of the *Enterprise* could give them.

Myra Coles, the computer had informed him, was one of the two elected leaders on Tyrtaeus II, although she had no title. Tyrtaeans, according to Federation records, did not bother with titles.

"There seems little need," Spock murmured, "to send the same message twice, especially since we acknowledged the earlier one."

"I think," Kirk said, "that they just want to remind us of how annoyed they are about this whole business, but without engaging in any unseemly displays of emotion. You have to admit that their earlier messages were masterpieces of a sort. I wouldn't have thought it possible to express so much anger and bad feeling in so few words, and so simply."

Spock lifted a brow. "The Tyrtaeans have a reputation for practicality. They would not have wanted to waste either our time or their own with a long message."

"Yet they'll waste time by sending it twice," Uhura murmured.

Spock glanced toward the communications officer. "They are human, Lieutenant, the descendants of settlers from Earth. That is undoubtedly enough to account for any apparent contradictions in their behavior."

Ouch, Kirk thought. *If I were in a pettier mood I could remind him that guessing games are illogical.*

But Vulcan guesses were pretty reliable, he reasoned. Especially Spock's guesses. Maybe it was the human in Spock that made him capable of his often brilliant intuitive leaps.

In any case, Kirk reminded himself that the triumph of Vulcan rationality had not been complete; traces of Vulcan's violent past could still be found in such customs as the *koon-ut-kal-if-fee,* or in the *kahs-wan* survival ordeal. Still, the Vulcans could be admired for the stability they had achieved, given the ferocity of their early culture. The Vulcans, unlike the Klingons—and unlike some human beings, Kirk reluctantly admitted to himself—had come to understand that violence was not something to glorify and celebrate. That was the way of the galaxy's intelligent life-forms; a net gain here and there, with the evolutionary legacy still in control, a dead hand guiding intelligences that were not yet ready to remake themselves and to be responsible for everything.

Kirk smiled inwardly. Spock himself had once said something much like that to him, in almost the same words. The Vulcan was not as naive as he sometimes seemed, and occasionally some warmth could be glimpsed in his usually impassive face. Naiveté was his way of keeping an open mind.

Spock exhaled softly, almost sounding as if he were sighing with exasperation, unlikely as that was. Kirk suspected that his science officer had even less enthusiasm for this routine mission than he did.

They were on their way to Tyrtaeus II to restore that planet's data base because of an unfortunate accident. During a routine update of the data bases of a few colony worlds, some Federation technicians had accidentally downloaded an old, long-hidden, and undetected virus along with the revised data. The virus had destroyed not only five planetary data bases but also the programs that ran the subspace communications systems of those worlds; new data bases could not be downloaded until the subspace systems were repaired on site.

The *Enterprise* had been going from one star system to another, repairing the subspace communications systems of each affected colony, then overseeing a new download from the Federation's database on Earth. That, Kirk thought, had been the easy part of a fairly tedious mission, which would at last be concluded on Tyrtaeus II.

The hard part was restoring the local history and recorded culture of each world, since that would have to come from other sources. Fragile and perishable documents had to be located, history and folklore rewritten and rerecorded, literature and poetry rediscovered and reproduced. After completing the straightforward work of repairs and downloads, all that Kirk and his personnel could offer was a certain amount of detective work. Some data could be recovered from the repaired data base and retrieval systems, but people trained in archaeology, historiography, and anthropology would have to ferret out the rest. The restoration would require a number of searches, and they had to face the possibility that some data might be permanently lost.

Spock had a theory, which he had been testing as often as practical, that the virus had not destroyed all of the data, but had merely "hidden" at least some of it. If he was even partially right, Kirk knew that a lot of hard work in search of physical records could be avoided.

The people on the four worlds that the *Enterprise* had already visited had been understandably irritated, even angry about the damage to their data bases. Kirk recalled how distressed the Lurissan Guides, the governing body of Cynur IV, had been when he had first met with them. The people of Cynur IV had a reputation as some of the warmest and most hospitable beings in the Federation; but the Cynurians Kirk had encountered had taken every opportunity to gripe and rail against the Federation for its carelessness; their hospitality had been grudging at best. He had no reason to expect the Tyrtaeans to be any more amenable, especially when they learned that perhaps not everything in their data base could be restored.

They also, Kirk reminded himself, had other reasons for not welcoming Starfleet personnel. Unlike the other four affected worlds, the Tyrtaeans had joined the Federation grudgingly. Their ancestors had left Earth a century ago; the Federation was a reminder of the world they had sought to escape.

Spock was still studying the strange object on the sensor screen.

"It's ironic," Kirk said. "The people of Tyrtaeus II pride themselves on withstanding adversity with forbearance. They scorn luxury, and think public displays of strong emotion are offensive. They have the reputation of being one of the more stoic and severe people in the galaxy. Now they are faced with a threat to their most ethereal artifact—their recorded culture. And that part of their civilization—the least practical and most unnecessary part—that is what they have complained about most keenly."

"I do not find that ironic, Captain," Spock said without turning from the screen. "What is most necessary for any being, all other things being given, is to maintain its identity, which is also essential to any culture. Irony, as I understand it, seems a superficial interpretation of the situation in this case. Least practical and most unnecessary is not how their loss should be described. What would you have the Tyrtaeans conclude? That they can do without what is apparently lost?"

Kirk considered for a moment. "You're right, of course. They might complain a bit less, though." He leaned closer to Spock to view the screen, where the heat signature of the mysterious object was still increasing. "We'll have to find out what that is," he added, "as soon as we've finished our job on Tyrtaeus II."

Spock nodded, as if approving of his curiosity,

then said, "I trust that it will be enough for the Tyrtaeans to learn that less was lost than they feared. It is fortunate that they overcame their reluctance and downloaded much of their data base in recent cultural exchanges. We will be able to restore all of what they downloaded at that time."

"Some of them won't be satisfied, Spock. Much of their cultural identity, as you say, was in those records."

"Kind of an insular culture," Uhura murmured, "from what the records indicate."

"No more so than those of some other colonies," Kirk said.

"But the Earth folk who came here wanted to be left entirely alone," Uhura continued. "According to our records, their admiration of self-reliance is so extreme that they seem to avoid any activity that might tempt them into dependence. They have less to do with other worlds than any other culture I can think of."

Kirk straightened. "We have to respect any colony's insularity, Lieutenant. Uniqueness can be inconvenient in the short run, but the Federation has to respect it if we're to have reliable cultural partners in future times. As Mr. Spock said, a culture's identity is essential, and must not be threatened."

"Quite right, Captain," Spock said, in what some would have regarded as a slightly patronizing tone; Kirk took the comment for what it was, a simple statement of fact. Spock was, he supposed, a superior being in a way. But not so much as to sever all bonds of sympathy with his comrades. Spock might strain those bonds of kinship, but they would never break.

As Captain Kirk turned away from the sensor display and resumed his post at his command station, Spock heard Lieutenant Kevin Riley say, "Entering standard orbit around Tyrtaeus II, Captain." Kirk nodded at the navigator, then waited for Lieutenant Sulu, who was seated at the helmsman's station on Riley's left, to confirm.

Spock gave only part of his attention to the routine activity on the bridge; he was looking back to his computer display screen as often as possible, where the heat signature of the unknown object was still increasing, telling him that the mysterious device was generating large amounts of energy.

"Standard orbit achieved," Hikaru Sulu announced from his forward station.

The bridge was oddly silent for a moment, Spock noticed.

"Mr. Spock," the captain continued, "are you with us?"

Spock was turning away from the screen when he saw a change on the long-range sensor scan. "Just a moment, sir," he murmured, leaning toward the screen again.

There was no doubt about it; the strange object had changed course.

"Captain," Spock said, "the unknown object I

have been observing has changed its orbit. It is now moving sunward, on what is clearly a collision course with the star."

"What?" Kirk said as he turned in his chair. "Then it definitely isn't a natural object."

"This is further confirmation that it is not natural."

Kirk frowned. "Lieutenant Uhura," he said, "open a hailing frequency to Tyrtaeus II."

"Hailing frequency open," Uhura announced.

The head and shoulders of a man appeared on the large bridge viewing screen. The man's face was lean and fine-featured, framed by short, dark hair. What Spock could see of his brown shirt was plain and unadorned. The man narrowed his eyes slightly, and his mouth twitched a little before he spoke.

"Aristocles Marcelli," the man said in a strained tone that Spock recognized as that of someone struggling to control his rage.

Kirk slowly got to his feet. "Aristocles Marcelli," the man said again in his flat voice, and Kirk quickly understood that the Tyrtaean was telling him his name.

"Captain James T. Kirk of the *Enterprise*," Kirk responded. "We're here to . . ."

"I know what you're here for." Aristocles Marcelli sounded merely irritated this time.

"Sir, we . . ."

"We don't hold with titles here, Kirk, even ones

like 'sir' or 'mister.' Call me Marcelli, or even Aristocles, if you like."

No greeting, no polite commonplaces, no attempt at even a semblance of warmth or courtesy. There was plain speaking, and there was rudeness; this man didn't seem to grasp the distinction.

"I trust that you'll be quick in replacing our loss," the Tyrtaean continued.

Kirk felt like a junior engineer reporting for nacelle cleaning duty. "We'll do our best—Marcelli."

"That kind of answer always sounds like an excuse in the making, Kirk. You don't anticipate any problems, do you?"

"We don't anticipate any problems beyond the ones we can reasonably anticipate," Kirk said.

"In other words, you're expecting some problems—just not any new problems."

The Tyrtaean seemed to be doing his best to be annoying, which did not seem consistent with the stoicism these people allegedly practiced. Kirk reminded himself that the reputedly friendly people of Cynur IV had only begun to warm to his personnel just before the *Enterprise* was to leave their system, and that all of the affected colonies had deeply resented the loss of their data bases. There had been no available target for their resentment other than the personnel of the *Enterprise*. Once again, Kirk decided to make allowances.

"As you well know," Kirk said, "we can't overcome the lack of physical backups. If you have lost certain kinds of data, we can't recreate that information from nothing. There has to be—"

"And who put us into this situation?"

Kirk kept his composure, although it was becoming more of an effort after dealing with the reproaches of four resentful worlds. "We'll do the best we can. I can promise you that, Marcelli. But we can't work miracles."

"Captain," Spock said, coming forward to face the viewscreen, "may I make a suggestion?"

Kirk glanced at him. "Of course." He motioned to Spock. "This is Commander Spock, my science officer and second-in-command of the *Enterprise.*"

Marcelli's brows shot up. "A Vulcan! Maybe now we'll get somewhere."

Kirk tried hard not to look annoyed.

"I do not wish to offer false hope," Spock said. "I merely wish to recommend that you do not give up on the physical presence of certain kinds of data. Such data may still exist in unexpected places on your world. For example, the inhabitants of Emben III were certain that several of their most highly prized narratives were lost. Records dating back to their earliest settlers were thought to have existed only in their damaged planetary database."

"Really," Marcelli said, sounding either skeptical or disappointed, it seemed to Kirk.

"He was practicing his calligraphy," Spock went on, "and preferred to do so while copying out old narratives by hand. So, whatever you have lost may still exist on your world, and possibly elsewhere, in surprising places. And I also suspect—"

"Tyrtaeans wouldn't waste time copying down old stories by hand," Marcelli muttered.

"And on Cynur IV," Kirk said, "a few people were quite upset at losing some poetry by one of their minor poets. As it happened, records of those poems had gone to the New Paris colonies as part of a cultural exchange. They were found in the personal library of a scholar who detested that particular poet and was in the middle of writing a devastating analysis of his poetry for a literary journal."

Aristocles Marcelli stared out coldly from the screen.

"In other words," Spock said, "do not limit your search only to the most logical places."

"A good thought, Spock," Marcelli said, and Kirk wondered if that comment might be a veiled insult to himself. Tyrtaeans might be stoic, but they were also apparently touchy. "I look forward to meeting you." The Tyrtaean did not sound as though he was including Kirk in that attempt at courtesy. "Needless to say, we've already started looking for physical sources of lost data, but we may have limited ourselves too much." A grimace that might have been an attempt at a smile passed across Marcelli's face. "Until we meet."

His image faded from the screen. "Seems he was unhappy," Kirk said as he sat down, "that he couldn't go on contending with us."

"We gave him few openings," Spock said.

"I suspect that he would be happier if you were in command of this ship."

Spock looked at him for a moment, obviously puzzled by the apparent jump in logical steps to a conclusion.

"In other words, my emotional control is akin to that of the Tyrtaeans, specifically to that of Aristocles Marcelli?"

"That's the general idea," Kirk said.

"Aristocles Marcelli and I are quite different, Captain. He is, after all, a human being. His steadfastness seems to me to be more an emotional insistence rather than a rational framework of being. The Stoic philosophers of your ancient world knew this quite well, the difference between wishing and knowing what is and what one can or cannot do about it."

"Thank you, Spock. I meant to express my admiration for the kind of deference you're able to elicit from these people. I don't seem to have the touch," Kirk said, barely suppressing a smile.

Spock nodded. "Thank you for explaining. It is very clear to me now."

"What is?"

"Why you suspected Aristocles Marcelli would be happier if I were in command. For the record, once again, I do not wish command, and will never seek it."

"But you would do it superbly."

"Of course."

Kirk thought about replying, then changed his mind. He tried to read the expression on his friend's face, but Spock was already moving aft, attracted by what the sensor display screen was revealing about that unknown object. Kirk was amused—and curious again, but he pushed those feelings aside. First things first.

Chapter Two

FROM THE FOOTHILLS of the Arrian Mountains, the city of Callinus looked to Wellesley Warren like a set of toy buildings arranged by an orderly child. The central square of the Tyrtaean municipality was clearly visible even from here; perfectly straight roadways ran from the corners of the square to the edges of the small city. The design resisted improvement whenever he saw it, and he had long ago given up on imagining its better, so pleasing was it to him.

"The first party from the *Enterprise* will be beaming down soon," Myra Coles said as she stood next to him.

Wellesley glanced at her and said, "We'd better go back, then," noting her flushed cheeks. She had obviously enjoyed the hike.

"Aristocles said he would be in the square with us to greet them, but he'll be expecting me to handle most of our subsequent dealings with them."

"He seemed very grateful when you volunteered to do so," Wellesley said.

"Yes—a little too grateful."

Wellesley knew what she meant. Myra's political position had been weakened by the loss of their world's data base, fueling the resentment of Tyrtaeans who already distrusted the Federation and who were beginning to see Myra as overly sympathetic to the Federation's interests. There were too many such Tyrtaeans, without whose support Aristocles Marcelli would never have been elected. He had played on their resentments during his campaign, reminding them of the settlers who had come here from Earth a century ago. They had seen back then what the United Federation of Planets would become, a network of cultures and worlds bound in interdependency, and they had wanted no part of it. Better to look out for oneself, and not count on anyone else.

Naturally, Aristocles would want Myra to manage the *Enterprise* personnel who would be restoring their data base. He would want to avoid the crewmembers as much as possible, so that if there were delays or any unexpected problems, he would be held blameless.

"We can go a little farther," Myra said, "before we head back."

He followed her up the hillside. Myra was ten years older than he was, but extremely fit; occasionally he had trouble keeping up with her. Like many Tyrtaeans, she did not care to hold meetings indoors when matters could be discussed outside, while getting needed exercise, and she had often led her aides on treks through the Arrian foothills. Improved circulation quickened their thinking, she claimed, enabling her to hear their best thoughts. Wellesley had been her aide for two years now, having joined her small staff of four right after graduating from Callinus's small university.

He used to wonder why Myra had selected him as one of her aides. He had been an outstanding student in both mathematics and history, but others had such qualifications. After his interview with her, he had not really expected to be chosen over older, more experienced people; he had feared that she might have glimpsed his secret self, despite his best efforts to keep his flaws hidden; he had been struggling with them all of his life.

"Wellesley is a daydreamer," his childhood teachers had said. "Wellesley is too demonstrative." "Wellesley mistakenly thinks of the classroom as a place for humor." "Wellesley must learn to avoid wasted effort and impractical pursuits." He had tried to overcome his flaws, but suspected that others still sensed them in him. He remembered worrying that he might have seemed too affable during his first interview with Myra. Now he suspected that she had chosen him because of his flaws, that she might even secretly share a few of his faults herself.

The aurora flowers of the foothills were in full bloom; their wide pink, salmon, and rose-colored petals covered the grassy slopes. The blue sky was cloudless, the air just warm enough for both of them to hike out here without jackets. He had often thought it ironic that the stern Earth folk who were their ancestors had settled such a hospitable planet, one with the kind of climate that might have led other settlers into hedonistic, indolent lives. With the Tyrtaeans, the invariably pleasant climate of their world's largest continent had only strengthened their isolationist tendencies: we have our world; we can get along by ourselves; we don't really need the Federation.

Unfortunately, the original settlers had made one mistake. By settling a world on the fringes of Federation space, they had believed that they had ensured their isolation. But the Tyrtaean system had turned out to be too close to the Neutral Zone to be left alone for long; the Federation had to make it clear to the Romulans that any foray into this system would be regarded as an act of war. Forty years ago, after a border skirmish with a warbird that got too close, the Tyrtaeans had unwillingly joined the Federation. They realized that was the only way to protect themselves if another war with the Romulan Empire ever came. Still, they had resented having to acknowledge such a dependence on the political entity they had hoped to escape.

Myra had been the Federation's advocate throughout her six years as one of her world's two leaders. "We value our independence, and the Federation allows us our independence," she had often argued. "Our isolation allows us to develop in our own way. But it also serves the Federation in the long-term. Some day, the Federation may need the culture we have developed, and we may need to strengthen our ties with our ancestral world. Then we will repay the Federation for its help, and free ourselves from what some mistakenly view as too much dependence upon it." Wellesley had never quite understood what she meant by that; it seemed to him that she was trying to have it both ways.

Still, Myra looked out from this world, to its future, but increasing numbers of Tyrtaeans seemed to be looking inward. Once, the Tyrtaeans who dreamed of founding a second colony, one far from this sector with no ties to the Federation at all, and of creating and keeping to a true Tyrtaean culture apart from any outside influences, had been a tiny group on the fringes of society. Now there were a quarter of a million of them, according to a survey Wellesley had conducted before their planetary data base had been lost, and even more who had some sympathy for their position. Time, these people cried, to sever all ties to the Federation, to settle another world where they would be left to themselves. They had been responsible for electing Aristocles Marcelli.

Myra stopped walking and turned toward him. "Let's hope that our data base is restored as quickly as possible," she said. "Any problems, and it's going to be even harder to convince the anti-Federationists that their way is a mistake." She let out a sigh. "They fear other cultures so much. Why can't they see that the kind of small colony they want wouldn't be viable, that such extreme isolation would only be setting themselves up for eventual failure? Why can't they understand that it's possible to love one's world and yet to try to look beyond it?"

Wellesley gazed at her in surprise; she was rarely so open and emotional, even with him, the only person with whom she shared her deepest thoughts. She looked away for a moment, then gazed back; her customary distant, almost severe, expression returned to her face.

"Enough self-indulgent outbursts," she murmured. "We must head back. I promised Aristocles I'd be with him to greet the first group of *Enterprise* officers. He'll be disappointed if I'm not there. He's probably getting tired of having to scold them all by himself."

Wellesley almost laughed, wondering if Myra had meant to make a joke, but she was frowning as she turned away and started back down the hill. It seemed to him that she was expecting trouble.

What she most feared was that the separatists might charge that the Federation had deliberately lost their world's data base, in an effort to retard the Tyrtaean culture's growth and development. There was not one bit of evidence to support the idea. Why would the Federation then be working so fast to restore all the lost data bases? The separatist rebels would have an answer for that also—to show how caring the Federation was, to elicit gratitude from their colonies, to draw them into greater dependency. Clever, but untrue, Wellesley told himself; but it sounded good and might convince many more people, if the charge were brought publicly—and then Myra's position would be even weaker, perhaps dangerously so.

When the transporter had cycled and she could see again, Uhura found herself in an open square of flat, bluish-gray rock, facing a large white structure that resembled Earth's Parthenon. This building, however, which housed the main library complex of Tyrtaeus II, was quite a bit taller than the ancient Greek monument; in fact, it seemed almost too tall to be supported by this particular type of architecture.

Commander Spock was already scanning the building with his tricorder. "The pillars have been reinforced," he said, "and also the inside walls."

"It's a lovely building," Uhura said. In spite of the buildings nearby, the library complex seemed to be standing in a kind of splendid isolation. She

23

looked around the square. Every building here was like that, she realized, part of a pleasing whole and yet very individual. There had been no attempt to make each structure a part of some overall design, and yet the square viewed as a whole had an austere beauty.

"The design of the library does have a classical simplicity," Ensign Tekakwitha murmured.

"That building there," Captain Kirk said, "with the walls that look like rose quartz—it's quite striking."

The architecture made Uhura think of their music. She had listened to some recordings of Tyrtaean compositions that the ship's computer had called up for her. The composers were clearly heavily influenced by Western neo-classical symphonies of the early twenty-second century, but there was something strange about the Tyrtaean symphonies. Uhura had listened to each performance twice before realizing why the music sounded so odd. The composition was more of a succession of solos rather than a symphony, with passages for string instruments, then for woodwinds, while the percussionists went their own way, resonating with the rest of the orchestra while still sounding independent of it. Given the way the music was written, Uhura thought, the musicians probably could have put on a performance without a conductor, which seemed consistent with the Tyrtaean approach to life.

The four officers had beamed down to the main

square of Callinus, the so-called Tyrtaean capital city. But to call it a city was an exaggeration; Uhura knew that fewer than forty thousand people lived in Callinus. The two million people on this world so prided themselves on their self-reliance that the vast majority of them lived in small villages, preferring them to larger cities that might rob them of some of their independence. But despite the Tyrtaeans' aversion to centralization, the library of Callinus was their cultural center, the repository of most of their society's treasured lore.

No wonder they were so bitter about the loss of their data base, Uhura thought. They must be as angry with themselves for their dependence on this library as they were of having any need of the Federation.

The other buildings surrounding the square were not quite as impressive as the library, but she admired them all. One long, low structure was made of a material that resembled cedar; at the other end of the square, across from the library, a massive stone stairway led up to the wide metallic doors of the Callinus Administrative Center. One door slid open; three people, two men and a woman, passed through it and descended the stone steps.

Uhura recognized one of the men as Aristocles Marcelli, so the woman with them had to be Myra Coles. The two Tyrtaean leaders had said that they would meet Captain Kirk and his landing party here. Myra Coles had been as terse as Aristocles

Marcelli in her messages, but Uhura had detected a softer note in her voice.

The three Tyrtaeans hurried across the square, slowing as they came closer, then stopped two meters away and stood rigidly, regarding the officers from the *Enterprise* with cool, disdainful expressions.

"Myra Coles," the woman said. Her thick chestnut hair was cut short, and she wore a simple gray tunic and trousers, but her kind of beauty needed no adornment. If anything, the plainness of her clothing only emphasized her attractiveness. Her large gray eyes were framed by thick dark lashes, and her flawless pale skin had a rosy glow; if the woman could ever bring herself to smile, Uhura was sure that she would see perfect white teeth.

"James Tiberius Kirk, captain of the *Enterprise*." The captain nodded at Myra Coles and smiled, clearly enjoying the chance to use his middle name; her mouth tensed, as if she resented his smile. "This is Commander Spock, first officer and chief science officer." Myra Coles stared at Captain Kirk without blinking; maybe she thought that even this scaled-down greeting was too effusive. "Lieutenant Uhura is our communications officer." He waved one arm toward Uhura, who smiled. "And Ensign Cathe Tekakwitha, one of our other science officers, is a trained anthropologist and information retrieval expert."

Ensign Tekakwitha was gazing at the Tyrtaeans as impassively as Spock. Uhura had worked closely with Cathe Tekakwitha when the ensign was first assigned to the *Enterprise,* and had been delighted to find that they shared an interest in ancient Egyptian art. She knew that the captain considered the young woman a promising officer, and Tekakwitha's quiet, dignified manner might help in dealing with the somber Tyrtaeans.

"Aristocles Marcelli," Myra Coles said, glancing at the other Tyrtaean leader. "But of course you've already met, so to speak." She looked uncertain for a moment, then motioned to the third man. "My aide, Wellesley Warren."

A quick smile passed across the face of the tall young man; he tugged at his mustache and quickly looked down, as if embarrassed by such a lapse. A Tyrtaean who actually smiled, Uhura thought; there had to be others like him.

"Our team of data retrieval experts is waiting in the library," Myra Coles continued. "We would like to get to work as quickly as possible, Kirk."

"So would we," Kirk replied. "We'll work as hard as possible to repay your kind reception."

Wellesley Warren made a noise that sounded suspiciously like a chuckle to Uhura, but the two Tyrtaean leaders seemed oblivious to the captain's mild sarcasm, and Myra Coles seemed immune to his charm.

"Let's hope that your hard work will be enough," Myra Coles said, and started to lead them toward the library.

"I know that you don't care for titles," Kirk said,

"but I'd prefer to address you as Myra rather than Coles."

"That's not necessary, Kirk. Everyone here except for my family, friends, and close associates calls me Coles."

"Call it an Earthman's affectation—and Myra is a lovely name." Uhura suppressed a smile at this comment of the captain's; Spock raised his eyebrow slightly.

"I don't care which of my names you use," Myra Coles said.

"And most of my friends call me Jim. If that strikes you as too informal, James will do."

"Very well, James. Since we're going to be working together, perhaps some cordiality will be appropriate."

Well, that's a start, Uhura thought. Maybe there was more warmth in the Tyrtaean woman than her culture allowed her to express.

"I think we're ready to run that test now," Christine Chapel said.

Leonard McCoy nodded at the nurse. They sat in one of the library's data retrieval areas; their small screens and consoles were set on a flat surface before them, linked to the library's data heads. The plain wooden furniture in the room lacked cushions, but provided some comfort along with support.

If all went well, McCoy thought, they would soon

be able to download the new medical data base. Annoying as it was to be working with this cursed machine, his job was relatively easy, certainly simpler than the work Lieutenant Commander Scott or Ensign Cathe Tekakwitha had to do. Scotty was in the basement chambers of the library with his engineers, installing new data modules while taking care not to lose any old data that might still be retrievable. Ensign Tekakwitha was in charge of the team that was working on the restoration of lost historical and cultural data; she had left that morning with Aristocles Martin and a few Tyrtaean historians to interview several older citizens for the library's oral history records.

Restoring the colony's medical data base presented no great difficulties. There was, as far as McCoy knew, no medical knowledge that was unique to Tyrtaeus II that had not already been taken by the Federation's subspace data harvesters. The Tyrtaeans should end up with exactly the same medical data base they had lost.

He had actually enjoyed his sessions with this world's physicians; once they got down to exchanging medical yarns, and notes about odd cases, he could almost forget that they were Tyrtaeans. Their records revealed that the average Tyrtaean was extraordinarily fit and healthy well into old age; these were not people inclined to indolence and self-indulgence. Usually they needed medical treatment only for injuries resulting from accidents or for illnesses that took a sudden unexpected turn for the worst, and almost all of them had acquired some knowledge of medicine, since they considered it foolish to be entirely dependent on a physician for medical treatment. The physicians here did not have many of the latest medical tools, but they were the sorts of doctors who did not like to rely too much on their instruments anyway, a quality McCoy could appreciate. He had developed a special liking for one old curmudgeon named Elliste who, like most of the medical personnel on this planet, had acquired great expertise in orthopedics. "Anybody who wants to know the upper limits of what human bones and joints can take ought to come here," Elliste had said, "because no Tyrtaean takes his aches and pains to a doctor until he's got no choice. I've seen folks who slapped on their own splints and homemade braces and just kept on going until they finished whatever they had to get done first."

McCoy's communicator beeped softly; he pulled it from his belt, snapped it open, and said, "McCoy."

"Scott here. You can start that test on the third section now, Doctor—those new data modules are up and running."

"We'll do that as soon as Christine's finished with the second section."

"Aye. Scott out."

It saved him and Nurse Chapel time to work

behind Scotty, running the tests after the engineer confirmed that each new section was ready to be checked. Both McCoy and Chapel knew as much about data base tests as they did about biological organisms. In two or three weeks, when all the modules were reset, the incoming subspace download would start. After that, the final tests would be run on the data directly from the *Enterprise* bridge, with the ship's computer.

"Computers can get ill just like people," Scotty had said to McCoy the other day. "Just feed them a lot of wrong ideas and wait for the flow of unexpected synergies to produce something that no one understands. And the closer a computer is to human capabilities, the sicker it can get."

If any further problems were encountered during these tests—always a possibility with these occasionally ornery computers—Tyrtaeus II would be without a usable data base for at least three weeks, possibly four. Apart from the physicians, the Tyrtaeans whom McCoy had met during his four days in Callinus had seemed increasingly irritable as time went on. He wondered what bothered them more—their dependence on their library's data base or their need for Starfleet's help in repairing the system.

McCoy concentrated on the screen in front of him, rechecking each module as Chapel ran the test. No glitches, no error messages—everything seemed to be going well. The damned machine was behaving itself today. He might as well be grateful for that, since this particular tour of duty had turned out to be even duller than expected. The people of Emben III, who had a reputation for histrionics, had certainly lived up to it while their data base was being restored; every small setback had resulted in public scenes of tears, recriminations, and bitter denunciations of the Federation's criminal carelessness by members of the Embenian Council. On Cynur IV, the normally cheerful and friendly inhabitants had gone out of their way to be rude. But at least those worlds had offered some diversions. The theaters of Emben III offered some of the best productions of Shakespeare to be found anywhere, and the Cynurians seemed to have a festival of some sort nearly every week. The Tyrtaeans of Callinus, from what McCoy had seen, did little except work, eat, and sleep.

Self-reliance, they called it. What was the point of a self-reliance that made a person try to emulate a machine?

"The second section is operational," Chapel announced, but McCoy had already noted that on his screen. By the time the two were finished running the tests on the third section of modules, Scotty had spoken to McCoy again over the communicator. The rest of his engineering team had beamed back to the *Enterprise;* he needed a break and a meal before the next round of work, and was going to see what the city of Callinus had to offer. McCoy and Chapel decided to join him.

They shut down their operations, left the data retrieval area, and entered the outside gallery. Scotty came toward them down the long, wide corridor, with Wellesley Warren at his side. McCoy could hear the young Tyrtaean's laughter even at this distance. The man had to be something of an eccentric and misfit by this world's standards; Wellesley Warren laughed easily, smiled more often, and didn't shy away from shaking hands or uttering a friendly greeting, as most Tyrtaeans did. But he was much more restrained when other Tyrtaeans came near, as if he could show his warmer nature only to the crew of the *Enterprise*.

Life here couldn't be easy for him, McCoy thought. Yet Wellesley Warren was also one of Myra Coles's trusted aides. If he had been able to win her respect, then obviously he had been successful at concealing qualities his people would see as weaknesses. It was puzzling, but maybe there were other relationships here that escaped the usual, and more than one Wellesley Warren.

"Where are we headed?" Christine Chapel asked as Scotty approached.

"Wellesley here advised us to try Redann's Tavern," Scotty replied. "It's just across the square."

"You could go to Doretta's Cafeteria if Redann's is crowded," Wellesley Warren said, "but it's three streets down, and, frankly, the food at Redann's is better. You'll be served—er, welcome there." McCoy reminded himself that there were places that would probably not welcome them. "Ask for the special—it's always the best thing on the menu."

"Coming with us?" McCoy asked.

"I have to meet with Myra and a team of historians." Warren was one of the people working on restoring lost cultural data. "Enjoy your lunch." The Tyrtaean hurried toward a staircase on their right.

"When's the rest of your team beaming back here?" McCoy asked Scotty.

"Most of them will be back this afternoon," the engineer said, "but Mister Spock needs a couple of engineers to work with him aboard the ship. He requested the two who are best at sensor system analysis and repair."

"He's already got Ali Massoud," McCoy said; Lieutenant Commander Massoud, a methodical young science officer who had won several commendations and also Spock's respect, was on duty with the Vulcan. "You'd think that would be enough help."

It had surprised McCoy that Kirk had sent Spock back to the *Enterprise* two days ago; the Vulcan and the Tyrtaeans seemed made for one another. But maybe the captain preferred to have his second in command aboard his ship, and Spock seemed anxious—if a Vulcan could feel anxious—to continue his observations of the unknown object, which was unexpectedly persisting in its sunward course.

"He's very curious about that thing," Nurse Chapel said.

"He sounded unusually interested when he spoke to me," Scotty said, "and if I didn't know better, I'd say he was even a wee bit worried about it."

Redann's Tavern, housed in a stone structure near the Callinus Administrative Center, turned out to be a large room filled with plain wooden tables and long benches.

"This is a tavern?" Scotty whispered as they sat down at a table near the back of the room. "Seems more like a study hall."

"Or a prison mess hall," Christine Chapel murmured.

"Maybe the food and drink will be worth it," McCoy said.

The waiter who took their order was a grim-faced man in a black tunic and trousers. He brought them three plates of meat and dark bread and three mugs of an amber-colored beverage, along with three knives.

McCoy made a sandwich of his meat and bread, cut it in half with his knife, and took a bite. The meat was well-cooked, probably boiled, without gravy or seasonings. "This is the special?" he said, keeping his voice low. "If this is the best dish on the menu, I'd hate to see the worst."

Christine Chapel took a bite of her bread, then

grimaced. "I had a childhood friend whose mother always used to complain that the foods that were best for you always seemed to taste the worst. She would have considered this bread very healthful."

Scotty sipped from his mug. "Tastes like watery tea. You'd think an establishment that calls itself a tavern would have something stronger to offer." He sighed. "These people make even Vulcans seem jolly."

McCoy chuckled, earning himself several blank stares from four men at a nearby table. "I don't think anyone here knows what a joke is," he said, then took another bite of his sandwich. "Well, here's one joke—this meat!"

"I don't know which is funnier," Scotty said with a straight face, "the food or the drink."

But the food satisfied McCoy's hunger, and the tealike beverage warmed his stomach and lifted his spirits a little, and he tried to think in a more fair-minded way. Maybe the Tyrtaeans weren't quite as dour as they seemed; maybe you had to get to know them before they loosened up. The physicians had certainly seemed more congenial while they were sharing their medical lore. Wellesley Warren was a friendly enough fellow, and there might be others like him. Myra Coles obviously respected her young aide; McCoy, during one meeting with them both, had seen how attentive she was to Warren's ideas about recovering lost historical data. Maybe she wasn't as cold and humorless as she appeared to be. Dig down deep enough, and no one knew much about anyone.

Kirk had been given quarters in a five-story hostel adjacent to the library. This building, which housed visitors to the capital city, was the closest Callinus had to a hotel, although it seemed more like a monastery. His small, bare room contained a narrow bed with a firm mattress, one shelf jutting out from a whitewashed wall, and a tiny closet. The lavatory, shared with anyone else staying on this floor, was at the end of the hallway. Uhura and Cathe Tekakwitha also had a room on this floor; except for having two shelves and two beds, it was exactly the same as his.

He sat on the bed to pull on his boots, then stood up. He and the other *Enterprise* officers on duty here did not really need quarters on the planet; he could come and go from the starship just as easily as he could walk over to the library complex. But Uhura had agreed strongly with him that it was best to accept the offer of hospitality, as they had on the other planets they had visited. To refuse might seem insulting, and the Tyrtaeans had seemed especially insistent. Perhaps, Uhura had surmised, the offer of a place to stay was also one of the few ways that the Tyrtaeans could demonstrate some friendliness.

"And there's another thing," the lieutenant had continued. "Have you noticed how it's almost always Myra Coles who deals with us, while Aristocles Marcelli keeps his distance? Cathe Tekakwitha says that whenever she has to work with him, he says as little as possible—hours can go by with hardly a word. Apparently a lot of his political backing comes from those who are hostile to the Federation, who think that they might be better off on their own."

"So what do you conclude?" Kirk asked.

"I suspect Coles is keeping the lid on."

Kirk knew of the separatists, and had endured an unpleasant encounter with a Tyrtaean data retrieval specialist whose son was a cadet at Starfleet Academy. Kirk had uttered some pleasantries about the respect the few Tyrtaeans serving in Starfleet had won for themselves during the short time their world had been a Federation member; the Tyrtaean man had scowled at him. "He didn't go with my approval, James Kirk," the man had replied, "and if he ever comes back here, I won't see him. Those young people go off, and once they've seen Earth and San Francisco, Tyrtaeus II and Callinus aren't good enough for them. Either they come back with a lot of impractical notions they picked up from other people, or they don't come back at all. That's one reason I think the anti-Federationists are right."

"Coles," Uhura went on, "may share a lot of her people's insularity, but she seems adamant about not leaving the Federation. She's probably the closest thing to an ally we have here."

"Which isn't saying much," Kirk murmured.

"I think she's trying, Captain. In any case, Marcelli seems ready to exploit any distrust of us that exists. That makes it even more important to be amenable to any suggestions Coles makes, and to accept all forms of hospitality. She needs all the help she can get."

Nonetheless, Kirk had diplomatically pointed out to Myra Coles that he did not want to put her people to any trouble, and that he and his crew could easily beam back and forth from the *Enterprise.* "And be dependent on the transporter?" she had replied, lifting a brow in the way Spock often did. "I don't think that's wise."

"We all have to depend on the transporter," Kirk had said.

"What if there's a malfunction? What if some glitch keeps you and your people from beaming back here?" Her voice had risen slightly, and he had reminded himself how unused to transporters these people were. To allow one's body to be converted into matter and beamed to a distant point was not something that came easily to Tyrtaeans; it required too much trust and dependence. "It might only delay the completion of your work here by a few hours or days while the transporter's repaired, but every day counts now," the Tyrtaean leader said more softly. "We must have our data base up and running as soon as possible."

He could not argue with that, accepting that restoring the data base quickly was the political achievement she needed most; but he had beamed back to the *Enterprise* on the sly a few times already. Sometimes, after a day spent in the company of Tyrtaeans, he just needed to see some smiling faces, and to unwind without having to worry that any friendly gesture might give offense. Of much more concern was the fact that Spock had become very curious about the enigmatic object that was moving toward the Tyrtaean sun. Kirk had begun to worry more about the object himself, even while trying to concentrate on the work of this mission; any unknown had to be regarded as a possible danger. It was already an important find; how important or dangerous waited to be determined.

Lieutenant Uhura and Ensign Tekakwitha would already be at the library. Kirk left his room and took the lift down to the small lobby. As usual, it was empty, and for good reason. It contained no furniture, as if the hostel's management wanted to make sure that no one would be tempted to loiter there. He reminded himself that he and his crew would not be on Tyrtaeus II much longer, a week or two more at most. Enduring oddities, irritations, and what seemed to be lapses in taste, would soon come to an end. Compared to some of their missions, this one could almost qualify as a vacation; he might as well take advantage of that.

The weather, as usual, was clear and dry, the air clean and cool. The Tyrtaeans certainly could not complain about their climate, Kirk thought. People strode through the square, backs stiff, eyes gazing straight ahead. Tyrtaeans moved as if they had no time to waste and knew exactly where they were going; he had never seen anyone wandering aimlessly, and even the children he saw on their way to classes had purposeful looks on their faces.

Kirk nodded in greeting, as he always did, to the people who passed him in the square. Most of the Tyrtaeans ignored him, but two men and a woman nodded back, and two boys hurrying past actually dared to smile.

As he approached the library, he thought again of Myra Coles. It was rare to meet a woman so unconscious of her own beauty—so much so that he did not have to fear that any graceful compliments or friendly gestures on his part might offend her, because she simply ignored them. She never let down her guard, even when he gave her his undivided attention, but he wondered if she might be a woman with banked fires. She seemed more at ease in the company of Wellesley Warren; a truly cold person would not have chosen that congenial young man as an aide.

There was no place to eat at the hostel, but the Tyrtaeans had set up food slots in a small room next to the library gallery for the *Enterprise* personnel and any Tyrtaeans working with them. Kirk helped himself to a late breakfast of a hot, brown beverage that smelled of chicory and a bowl filled with a substance that resembled gruel. McCoy was just getting up from a table with Wellesley Warren;

the doctor muttered something under his breath and Warren laughed. The two men clearly got along; Kirk had often seen them together.

"How's it going, Bones?" Kirk asked.

"My job's done," McCoy replied. "I'm going over to the Administrative Center to meet with some physicians, but that's mostly to see if they've got any more local medical lore that I should know about."

"And we've found those two journals by early settlers we thought were lost," Warren said. "An old woman in Teresis—that's a town near here—has copies. Myra sent me a message about it this morning."

"Glad to hear it," Kirk said.

"You and your people won't have to stay here much longer. Still, we'll be sorry to see you go."

Kirk doubted very much that most of the Tyrtaeans would be sorry to see him and his crew leave, but it was courteous of the man to say so. "We'll have to pay you a return visit sometime," Kirk replied, just to be polite.

There had been many times, he told himself as he sat down, when it had been a struggle to keep himself from making a humorous remark that he knew the Tyrtaeans would take seriously. Dealing with such somber, earnest people, taking care not to insult them with remarks that might seem flippant to them while reminding himself that their blunt speech and expressionless stares were not intended as rudeness—he had been tempted to order Lieutenant Riley to beam down just to see how the Tyrtaeans would react to his sprightly and irrepressible personality. The overwhelming conclusion he had drawn about the Tyrtaeans was that they just didn't have to be the way they were, but persisted in their ways out of sheer stubbornness.

Uhura and Cathe Tekakwitha came into the room; the lieutenant nodded at him. The two women helped themselves to cups of the chicory-flavored beverage, then came over to his table.

"Good news, Captain," Uhura said as she sat down. "We're just about finished installing the subspace communications components. We've already started running tests, and we should be ready for the incoming subspace download this afternoon."

Kirk heard the note of relief in her voice, and said, "Then our job's nearly done."

"Yes." Uhura sighed. "I'll be glad when this mission is over. I certainly don't intend to offer any more musical performances before we leave."

"Musical performances?" Kirk asked.

"Two evenings ago," Tekakwitha said, "a group of us were walking back to the hostel, and we decided to stop for a drink at Redann's Tavern. Then somebody—I think it was Ensign Marais—said that what we needed was some music."

"So I went across the square to the hostel," Uhura said, "to get my Vulcan harp, and when I went back to the tavern and started to play—" She paused, looking exasperated. "I never saw such icy stares. Believe me, I didn't play for very long. It wasn't that anyone was complaining—they just stared at me without reacting at all."

"Wellesley Warren was with us," Tekakwitha said, "and two other Tyrtaeans." She shook back her long, black hair. "They assured us that Lieutenant Uhura wasn't doing anything offensive—in fact, they seemed as anxious to hear her play and sing as our crewmates were. Wellesley was very apologetic—said that people here just aren't used to hearing music in a tavern."

"Imagine not knowing what to make of music in a tavern," Uhura murmured.

"I sympathize," Kirk said with a smile. "I've had Myra Coles and aides of Aristocles Marcelli complaining at me one minute for any delays, and then muttering about their resentment at needing our help at all."

"Tyrtaeans are obsessively self-reliant," Tekakwitha said, "and controlling. They almost make a fetish of it."

"I suppose that's better than being weak and cowardly," Kirk said.

Tekakwitha smiled. "I keep reminding myself that their ways aren't our ways, and that we have to respect that. And Federation colonies have to be insular in order to develop their own cultures. When they're more secure, they'll reach out. The Federation's strength is in its diversity, and we may have great need of Tyrtaean mores in time, what they've developed in their isolation from other cultures—that quality they have of acting as if they have to stand up to whatever the universe throws at them."

Kirk nodded. The ensign was not just speaking as an anthropologist, he knew, but as a Mohawk. Her own people had needed time to relearn their old language and practice their customs apart from the white European culture that had nearly overwhelmed them, and they were stronger for having withdrawn for a period. Too bad that the Tyrtaeans had to be so dull and dogged about it.

"Maybe you should have kept Mr. Spock down here," Uhura said. "The Tyrtaeans might have found his manner more to their liking."

Kirk was not so sure. Many of the Tyrtaeans might have found Spock extremely irritating after a while, a reminder that they, for all their restraint, could never be as controlled as a Vulcan. Spock had also implied that, for all their Spartan customs and behavior, he found the Tyrtaeans quite illogical for harping on the need for self-reliance when they so clearly needed Starfleet's help. Resentment of the Federation for an unforeseen, accidental error seemed equally illogical to him. Sensing that Spock might prove to be more of an irritant than a balm to the people here, and knowing how curious he was about the object coming in from the outer solar system, Kirk had decided it was best to leave him in charge of the *Enterprise.*

Uhura took another sip from her cup, then set it down. "Well, back to work."

As she got to her feet, Kirk's communicator sounded. He pulled it from his belt and flipped it open. "Kirk here."

"Captain," Spock's voice said, "I have important news." Uhura sat down again; Tekakwitha leaned forward. "The unknown object is still on a course for the sun. Our most recent scan indicates that there are life-forms aboard. They have not responded to any of the standard hailing frequencies. If the object continues on its present course, it seems likely that any life-forms aboard will perish."

"Does it show any sign of changing course?" Kirk asked.

"None, Captain. I suspect that if there is intelligence aboard, it may have lost control of its vessel. Or it may be deliberately aiming for the sun—for what reason, I cannot conjecture. The object is too distant for us to do deep scans."

"We're just about finished here," Kirk said, feeling a twinge of apprehension. "It's time we took a closer look at this curiosity. I know it's been working on your mind."

"It is most intriguing."

"Any ideas of what it might be?"

"I would rather not speculate," Spock said. "There is a much better way."

"And what is that?" Kirk asked, instantly realizing that he wasn't thinking, that he already knew the answer to his question.

"To go and see," Spock said.

Uhura laughed softly. "Obviously," Kirk replied irritably. He was in no mood for Spock's version of a witticism.

"Not obviously, Captain," Spock said. "I have seen too many human beings, both past and present, who seem to prefer guessing to learning."

Kirk did not take the bait. "Guessing games are not on the agenda today, Mr. Spock. Prepare to investigate the object. Kirk out." His communicator closed with a satisfying snap. He could hardly wait to be done repairing planetary data bases. Necessary as the mission was, it had gone on long enough; it was putting him to sleep. A real challenge was just what he needed now.

Chapter Three

MYRA COLES was just about to call Aristocles Marcelli on his private line when her phone buzzed. She opened the line and Aristocles's recorded voice said, "I am requesting that we have a private meeting at my quarters within the hour. Thank you."

As she closed the line, it became obvious to her that he was anxious, but she wondered whether that was the impression he wished to create or one that had slipped out of his control. So often had Aristocles Marcelli worked to keep her off balance that she could not imagine him losing any of his self-control. Still, it was possible, given the situation and the stakes. She would have to be alert during their meeting to any confirming clues. They would be crucial to her political survival.

* * *

Aristocles's house, at the southern end of Callinus, was an almost ostentatiously plain one-story building of wood and glass. He greeted Myra at the door and ushered her into a room furnished only with three cushions and a low wooden table.

She had brought a small bag of sewing with her. She settled herself on one of the cushions and took out a shirt with seams that needed stitching. No sense in recycling a shirt that could still be mended and worn; no point in sitting here and talking while her hands were idle. Some tools were laid out on the table, along with a small portable appliance Aristocles was apparently in the middle of repairing.

"I'm very curious about that object in our outer system," Aristocles said as he fitted a component to the side of the appliance, "and I suspect you are, too."

"Of course," she said carefully. "I'm sure that James Kirk and his people will want to find out more about it."

"We must recommend that they take a good look at the artifact, and share all their observations with us. In fact, I think it might be wise to have an observer of our own aboard the *Enterprise* when it goes out to meet whatever this is."

Myra paused in the middle of a stitch. She had wanted to make the same recommendation. It bothered her that he had anticipated her actions, that he wanted the same thing she did.

"This is our planetary system," she said. "We do have the right to find out about this unknown object and what it may mean to us."

"Exactly. I think that you, and one of your aides, should be a part of any exploration. Frankly, I can't think of anyone better for the job."

She drew her needle through the shirt, keeping her eyes down. She had intended to ask for that, too. All afternoon, she had been thinking of how to make such a suggestion to Aristocles, who was so deeply resentful at having any dealings with Starfleet, the Federation's arm; but she had worried about playing into his hands.

And, she admitted to herself, she was not anxious for more prolonged contact with Starfleet officers. She had found her few past encounters with Starfleet trying, even though she knew that Federation membership was in her world's best interests. The last Federation envoy to come here three years ago had treated her as someone he could not entirely trust. The treaty they had crafted together had preserved the autonomy of her world while leaving the way open to communication and closer future ties to the Federation. But forging the agreement had drained her, and many Tyrtaeans had seemed hostile to her efforts.

Aristocles Marcelli had won election in the aftermath of the treaty she had negotiated, so she had put aside her more self-indulgent feelings. He would try to undo everything she had accomplished if she did not stand against him.

"We have our pride, you know," Aristocles went on. "You have noted, of course, that James Kirk didn't tell us about his science officer's discovery until we brought up the fact, following the reports of our own observers. He probably would have informed us, but we can't know that now, can we? Still, Kirk and his people *did* restore our data base. The least we can do to repay them is to offer to help in investigating that mysterious object."

How disingenuous he was. Myra lifted her head. Aristocles shifted his slender body on his cushion, averting his eyes from her as he fitted another component to his appliance.

I know what you want, she thought; you want me on the *Enterprise* so that you won't be contaminated by too much contact with nonTyrtaeans, with people who have embraced all that our ancestors abandoned. You want me there if anything goes wrong, in case this object proves to be a danger. Maybe I'll make a mistake in judgment, and give you even more reason to criticize the Federation and those Tyrtaeans who value our membership in it, who trust the Federation too much. That would strengthen your position, and might fatally weaken mine.

But perhaps she was supposing too much, too quickly. There was no reason as yet to think that the unknown object posed any danger, and it would be appropriate to have someone aboard the

Enterprise to look out for Tyrtaean interests. And she, Myra admitted to herself, was the most qualified person to go.

She was wary of James Kirk, the starship captain, a man too free with courtly gestures and compliments; his company, she grudgingly admitted to herself, could become too pleasant if she allowed it. Aboard his ship, her fate would be in his hands. She would have to make it clear—would have to remind herself—that her responsibilities to Tyrtaeus II were her highest priority. Nothing, and especially not her curiosity about the discovery, could override that responsibility.

"I agree with you," she said. "Let's settle on exactly what we'll say, then ask for a meeting with James Kirk as soon as possible." She wished that she could quiet her suspicions, rid herself of the feeling that she was saying exactly what Aristocles Marcelli had planned.

Their task was done, and as Kirk had hoped, nearly all lost data had been restored to the Tyrtaean data base. A few early historical accounts were still missing, along with some bits of folklore, but Wellesley Warren already had clear leads as to where these might be found.

Kirk had intended to beam up to the *Enterprise* from his room, but Myra Coles and Aristocles Marcelli had asked to meet with him in the hostel's lobby. Perhaps they simply wanted to mark his departure with some kind of gesture or ceremony, unlikely as that was for Tyrtaeans. Maybe they were only preparing to thank him and his crew for their efforts.

Kirk was moving toward his door when his communicator sounded. He flipped it open. "Kirk here."

"Captain," Spock's voice said, "I have just received a message from Myra Coles telling me that she and her associates have requested a meeting with you."

"I'm on my way to it now."

"They have requested my presence at that meeting as well. I am in the transporter room preparing to beam down."

"No reason for you not to be there, Spock. They're probably planning some show of a farewell for us, and maybe they thought that my first officer should be included." He hoped that was all it was, but his instincts were already telling him that the two Tyrtaean leaders had something else in mind. Asking Spock to beam down simply to go through the motions of saying thank you and good-bye did not seem like something the eminently practical Tyrtaeans would do. "I'll meet you in the lobby. Kirk out."

The door slid open. Uhura and Tekakwitha were waiting for him by the lift; since they had spent more time on the planet than almost anyone else in his crew, he wanted them present at this last encounter.

The lift whisked them to the first floor; they emerged to see Spock standing in the lobby with Myra Coles and Aristocles Marcelli. Wellesley Warren stood to the right of Myra Coles.

The four were silent as Kirk and the two female officers crossed the lobby. Even Wellesley Warren seemed uncharacteristically solemn. Kirk stopped in front of the group; they seemed to be waiting for him to speak first.

He cleared his throat. "I'd like to say," he said, "how pleased we are that so little of your local data was lost. The Federation's librarians and computer technicians have learned a lot from this mistake, and the Council has asked me to assure you that such incidents are highly unlikely to happen again." He waited, hoping that the Tyrtaeans could bring themselves to utter a simple expression of thanks.

"You've done your job well," Aristocles Marcelli said in a toneless voice. "That's not why we wanted to meet with you. We're concerned about that object that is now moving through our outer solar system, and strongly recommend that you go and investigate it."

"That's exactly what we were preparing to do," Kirk replied. "One of our directives is to take the initiative in investigating unknowns, as long as another mission does not take precedence." That sounded official enough. He glanced at Spock, who gazed back at him without expression.

"I assume that Spock has been collecting data about this object," Myra Coles said, "since he is your science officer, and he has remained on your ship during most of this mission."

"Yes," Kirk said, "—along with his other duties."

"You might have shared those observations with us," Marcelli said, "instead of leaving us to duplicate your efforts. When did you realize that it probably wasn't a Romulan artifact?"

"Before we entered orbit around this planet," Spock replied.

"You might have told us then, instead of leaving us to draw that conclusion ourselves." Marcelli scowled. "The protection you offer us from the Romulans was the only practical reason for joining your Federation. But perhaps you wanted to leave us in doubt for a while, so that we'd be more grateful to you."

Myra Coles turned toward Spock. "Does this object pose any danger to our world?"

"I cannot tell you that with absolute certainty," Spock replied, "but its present course will keep it at a safe distance from this planet."

"Exploring that object is our next priority," Kirk said. "Naturally, we'll make certain that you're informed of anything we find out."

"That isn't all that we want." Aristocles Marcelli lifted his chin slightly. "We insist upon sending two of our people along on this mission."

Kirk stiffened. "That isn't necessary."

Myra Coles narrowed her eyes. "James," she said, "may I remind you that this is our home system? We have the right to explore it or to participate in its exploration."

"That's true enough." Kirk tried to keep his voice low, but firm. "But Federation members do not have the right to invite themselves aboard Starfleet vessels."

Spock tilted his head toward the captain in apparent agreement, but he did not speak.

"May I remind you," Aristocles Marcelli said, "that the physical and mental rigors of our educational system here produce people as tough and disciplined as any Starfleet Academy graduates. I don't think you'll find our people an undue burden." He shot an irritated look at Spock, who lifted his eyebrows in response.

"You came here to help us," Myra Coles said. "You succeeded. We are now offering to assist you in turn, and you should know by now that we wouldn't be making such a request if we didn't think we could be of help." Her gray eyes gazed at Kirk steadily.

So this was also a matter of pride, Kirk thought, an attempt at repayment for the repair of their data base. Or was it? "Exactly whom do you want us to bring along?" he asked.

"We propose," Aristocles Marcelli said, "that you take along Myra Coles and Wellesley Warren.

Myra's training as an astrophysicist might be of use, and both she and Wellesley have had experience in exploring the uninhabited and more isolated regions of Tyrtaeus II. In addition, they've both worked closely with you and your crew during the past weeks. That should make it easier for them to adapt to life aboard your starship."

About Wellesley Warren, the least tiresome of Tyrtaeans, Kirk had few doubts. He was somewhat more dubious about Myra Coles.

"And precisely what would their function be?" Spock asked.

"They would be observers," Aristocles Marcelli replied. "You might find their observations and advice helpful."

"We won't interfere with the mission," Myra Coles said, "and shall remain under your command at all times. If you feel that either of us is an impediment, impose the same discipline on us as you would on any of your crew." Her mouth moved, as if she were about to smile and then thought better of it. "I assure you that we won't be a problem."

"Very well," Kirk said. "You may come aboard the *Enterprise*. We'll be leaving orbit at oh-seven-hundred your time, so be prepared to beam up at oh-six-hundred."

Myra Coles nodded. "Thank you, James—for that, and for your efforts here."

Kirk sighed inwardly. At least he and his people

had finally been thanked. "I'll give you my first order now. I know that your people disdain titles, but I must insist that you follow formal Starfleet protocol while aboard. That will make things easier for all of us."

"Of course—Captain," Wellesley Warren said quickly.

"Lieutenant Uhura and Ensign Tekakwitha will remain with you until you're ready to beam aboard, and will answer any questions you may have about how to conduct yourselves aboard the *Enterprise.*" He pulled out his communicator. "Kirk here—two to beam up. Myself and Mr. Spock."

The lobby faded; Kirk found himself in the transporter room. Transporter Chief Kyle was on duty; he looked up from his console. "Welcome aboard, sir."

"Prepare to beam Uhura, Tekakwitha, and two Tyrtaean observers aboard from Callinus in four hours," Kirk said as he stepped down from the transporter.

"Captain," Spock said as he reached Kirk's side, "I think you were wise to avoid a confrontation with the Tyrtaean leaders. However, our two guests will almost certainly be unnecessary."

"I know, Spock. But it is politic to consider their pride. And who knows, perhaps they will make themselves useful after all."

"Useful, possibly, since their culture places such

value on constructive activity, but unnecessary all the same, given that members of the crew could perform any tasks you might assign to them. And this pride of theirs—I take it that you admire it?"

"I suppose I do. It makes up a little for their shortcomings in other departments."

"Admiration is hardly a sufficient reason to bring Myra Coles and Wellesley Warren aboard."

Kirk rubbed his tired eyes. It was a good thing that Spock didn't question his decisions often. Even Vulcans weren't usually this stubborn.

"If I hadn't agreed to take them aboard, Myra Coles and her colleagues might have sent a protest to the Federation Council," Kirk said patiently. "Chances are that the Council and Starfleet would have taken my side, but they also would have been critical of me for not doing more to ease the hard feelings here, especially with a sizable part of the population wanting to cut themselves off entirely from the Federation. And if Myra somehow persuaded them to take her side, we'd have to bring her and Wellesley aboard anyway. It's simpler to allow them to come aboard and inform Starfleet of my decision. If they create any problems for us, they'll be restricted to quarters for the duration of the mission. At worst we can send them back in a shuttlecraft."

"And no one would object to such an action at that point," Spock said. "I cannot fault the logic of your diplomacy, Captain."

Kirk offered a wan smile. After all of his dealings with the Tyrtaeans, it was nice to receive a compliment—even a reserved Vulcan compliment.

"Nevertheless, we must consider the possibility that this is some part of a planned provocation."

Kirk sighed. So much for compliments. "We'll see," he said as they entered the turbolift.

Hikaru Sulu brought the *Enterprise* closer to the mysterious planetoid, then leaned back from his console. The starship was following the object in a parallel orbit as it continued on its long plunge toward the sun. At Sulu's right, Kevin Riley was gazing intently at the bridge viewscreen.

Sulu lifted his eyes to the viewscreen. The object appeared to be a common asteroid, but an unusually symmetrical one; most asteroids looked like lumpy gray potatoes. This one was rocky, with some nickel iron, and its surface was pockmarked from eons of collisions with smaller objects.

"Lieutenant Uhura," Captain Kirk said behind him, "run through all hailing frequencies."

"Now running," Uhura replied from her station.

The life-forms that had been detected aboard the object during approach were still failing to respond, or else for some reason had not yet picked up any signals from the *Enterprise*. The second possibility, Sulu knew, was highly unlikely at this distance; surely they were aware of the starship's presence by now. Could it be that they were simply *choosing* to remain silent?

"Plotting the course of the object," Riley said. "Here's something curious, Captain. The object seems to be making course adjustments that will bring it on a collision trajectory with the sun."

"Are you sure, Lieutenant Riley?" Kirk asked.

"Our course is maintaining relative position to the object, and we're following its lead."

"Any clues yet as to what kind of life-forms are aboard it?" Kirk said.

"Negative," Commander Spock replied from his station. "We have nothing in our records of alien life-forms with which to compare the data our sensors have picked up from this object."

"What kind of propulsion is at work?" Kirk asked.

"Unknown," Sulu said, "but it's obviously some kind of field-effect system, pushing at a low level right now."

"And the energy source?"

"I can't detect one," Sulu said, "so it must be completely shielded. But that's only an assumption, because I can't detect any shielded areas, either."

"Strange," Riley muttered.

Sulu heard the lift door open. He looked over his shoulder and saw Yeoman Janice Rand come out on the bridge, followed by Myra Coles and Wellesley Warren, the Tyrtaeans the captain had allowed aboard. Those two didn't give away much, Sulu thought. They had come to the bridge with Uhura and Tekakwitha just after beaming aboard. Kirk had quickly introduced them before sending them off for a routine medical exam and settling them into their temporary quarters. They had smiled uneasily at everyone on the bridge, keeping their arms stiffly at their sides.

But Sulu had immediately seen why the captain might want to get to know Myra Coles better. She was, he admitted, a beautiful woman, plainly dressed and unadorned as she was. Still, Captain Kirk would not have brought her aboard only because he found her attractive, and she and her aide had seemed anxious to assure the crew that they would be of use.

Yeoman Rand led the two Tyrtaeans to the captain's station and murmured a few words to him. Myra Coles lifted her head and looked toward the screen, clearly intrigued by the unknown object. She wouldn't have asked to come aboard only out of curiosity, Sulu thought. He suspected that she was worried, although she was doing a good job of concealing any feelings of fear. Any unknown could be a threat, and this particular unknown was insisting on remaining mysterious.

"Miss Coles and Mister Warren." Kirk got to his feet. "Perhaps you'd like to see what it feels like to sit at the command point of a starship."

Wellesley Warren sat down at the captain's chair, grinned with pleasure, then looked solemn again.

"Thank you, Captain," he said. "May I join your science officers now?" He glanced up at Spock and Lieutenant Commander Ali Massoud. "I'd like to study the data they've already acquired about the object."

"Permission granted."

Warren got up and walked toward Spock's station; Myra Coles gazed warily at the captain's chair.

"Do sit down, Miss Coles," Kirk said, waving an arm at his station. "You should feel at ease here, as one of the leaders of a world. After all, I am only captain of this ship."

Myra Coles flushed, then sat down.

"I trust that your quarters are satisfactory," Kirk continued.

"More than adequate," she said, "and your chief physician has pronounced us both in good health." She paused. "I am sorry that three of the people who gave us so much help are in sickbay now."

Kirk smiled. Myra Coles wore her usual serious expression, but at least she was trying to be gracious. "Doctor McCoy and his staff will have them on their feet again soon."

"Yeoman Rand was most cordial while showing us around your ship." The Tyrtaean woman grimaced slightly, as if displaying such courtesy was a continuous effort. "She mentioned in passing that you are a man who appreciates the company of women."

"I see," Kirk said lightly.

"I am sure that women appreciate your company as well."

Kirk tried hard not to smile as he glanced at her. He almost succeeded.

"You occasionally behave in what I think you would call a 'courtly' manner, are obviously quite intelligent, and wouldn't be a Starfleet officer if you didn't have exceptional abilities—and your appearance is not displeasing."

She was looking straight at him as she spoke, but he couldn't be sure if she was trying, however awkwardly, to flirt, was stating what she believed to be facts, or was mocking him. "I appreciate the compliments," Kirk said.

"I am not given to flattery." Her mouth curved up, and for a moment he thought that she would smile. "We have a saying on my home world, Captain. 'A man alone is self-reliant, and reliable.' I must conclude, therefore, that your own reliability is questionable."

She had spoken the words softly; he did not think that she meant to insult him. "But I am alone," Kirk said, too quickly.

"No, you are not. You have your ship."

She had seen into him, and her gray eyes were gazing at him more warmly. Maybe she thought more of him than he realized; that might have to do with her seeing that he loved something more than himself, as she probably loved shepherding her people through the mazes of political life.

Myra Coles stood up. "We have spoken long enough. What can I do now to be of use?"

"I suggest that you join your aide and my science officers. Maybe you'll see something in the data we haven't spotted."

He gazed after her as she crossed the bridge, then sat down. The asteroid was still on the viewscreen, still moving toward the sun, its life-forms still refusing to communicate.

"McCoy to bridge. Jim?"

"Mind if I come up to the bridge and take a look at that alien object?" McCoy asked.

"Permission granted," Kirk said, and turned back to the viewscreen.

McCoy hurried from the lift, nodded at the two Tyrtaeans, and then came toward Kirk's station, scowling even more than usual.

"Take a look, Bones." Kirk gestured toward the viewscreen.

McCoy stared at the screen for a while in silence. "What in blazes is that thing out there, anyway?" the physician asked.

"That," Spock said from his station, "is what we are attempting to find out."

"Well, I know that, Spock." McCoy shook his head. "What I meant was, how do we know it's worth bothering about?"

"We do not know that, either," Spock said. "We will have to go inside it to find out anything more."

Kirk had already come to that conclusion. McCoy frowned as he stared at the viewscreen. "That thing worries me. I don't much care for mysteries, especially ones where you get so few clues." He was silent for a moment. "You aren't seriously thinking of going inside it, are you?"

"That may be necessary," Kirk said. Myra Coles drew her brows together; he wondered if she would insist on coming along.

"Let's just hope you don't pick up something a lot worse than indigestion, then." McCoy rubbed his chin. "I don't like the idea of going inside something we know so little about."

"We'll take the usual precautions."

"Our sensor scan indicates that there is breathable air inside the object," Spock said. "I recommend that we enter it and see if we can contact the life-forms from the inside. There is no obvious sign of danger."

"Except that the life-forms are uncommunicative," McCoy said, turning toward Spock. "Doesn't that tell you anything?"

"Only that they are unable or unwilling to respond to our messages," Spock replied. "It doesn't necessarily indicate that they are a danger to us. They may be incapacitated."

"Occam's razor," Kirk said. "In the absence of evidence, don't conclude anything. Not quite what Occam said, but in the same spirit."

"I must advise against entering that asteroid. We

should gather as much information as possible before going inside."

Kirk paused. First McCoy, now Myra. Who else was going to get into the act? "We may not have time to do that. Let me remind you that there are alien life-forms inside, and that worldlet is still heading sunward. If it doesn't change course, those life-forms will die. We have to find out more to have any chance of preventing that. We've got to find a way to communicate with them."

"If you go inside," she said, "how do you know that those life-forms won't interpret that as an act of aggression?"

"We can't be certain they won't," Kirk said, "but we have no evidence that they will. If they were truly fearful of us, they could have hidden in your solar system until we warped out of here. Assuming that they may be incapacitated seems more plausible. Ours may be an errand of mercy."

Myra Coles drew herself up. "You may be right. But I still strongly advise against going inside. I want that on the record, Captain."

"Noted," he said.

"Affirmative," the computer announced.

"And if you do go inside," the Tyrtaean woman continued, "who will you bring along?"

"Spock, of course. I haven't decided whether we need a larger party."

"A Tyrtaean should be part of the team, too," she said.

Politics, Kirk thought. On the one hand, a protest against going inside on the record, but on the other, a Tyrtaean as part of any exploratory team; she wanted to be covered both ways. The woman had a way of becoming especially irritating just as he thought they might be starting to get along.

Wellesley Warren and Spock were watching them. Ali Massoud frowned as he stroked his beard. Myra Coles glanced around the bridge, then looked back at Kirk. "But you are in command here, Captain," she continued, "and I leave that decision to you."

He was relieved that she was not going to challenge his authority openly, so he held back a sarcastic thank you to Myra for letting him run his own ship.

"We're going inside," he said at last. "I'll pick the team."

When Kirk went off duty, he asked Spock to meet with him in the briefing room. As the door slid shut behind the science officer, Kirk said, "Now that our Tyrtaean guests have volunteered for this mission, I'm inclined to bring one of them along, for diplomatic reasons, if nothing else. We have little reason to assume that exploring the object's interior poses any danger, despite what Myra Coles said, but it should be a simple matter to beam anyone out of harm's way if necessary."

"Wellesley Warren would be my choice, Captain," Spock said. "He is both intelligent and cooperative, so even if he is not of much use to us, he is unlikely to be a hindrance. As an astrophysicist, Myra Coles would be more useful assisting Lieutenant Commander Massoud and the other science officers aboard the *Enterprise*. Also, since she is one of the leaders of her world's government, she may be called upon suddenly for consultation on matters there. She should remain available to her people."

Kirk had been thinking the same thing, but was glad to hear it from Spock. Myra Coles could not object, given that she prided herself on her practicality.

"Very well," he said, surprised at how relieved he felt that Myra Coles would remain safely aboard the *Enterprise*. Strange, he told himself, that he should feel so relieved. Was it simply knowing that he would not have to contend with her thorny personality while exploring the worldlet's interior? Either he was more concerned about the woman than he had thought, or his instincts were warning him that a venture inside the object might be more perilous than he expected.

Expect the unknown, they had taught him at the Academy, until you sense its approach. He had loved the idea of it, but later they had told him how unreliable such feelings might be; that the genuine unknown would be completely unexpected, and that when it came it might remain forever unknowable. And the only advice he got was do the best you can, and break as few rules as possible.

Somewhere in those words, Kirk could hear, even now, an additional phrase: break as few rules as possible; make it look like you didn't—but make sure you're right.

Chapter Four

"I STRONGLY ADVISED against going inside the alien artifact," Myra said. "My objection is on record. I argued that more information should be gathered first, and that the life-forms inside the mobile may regard any intrusion as a provocation."

The impassive face of Aristocles Marcelli gazed out from the small screen in front of her. Myra was speaking to him over a secure channel from the quarters assigned to her by the captain. She might have simply recorded a subspace report for him to view later, but her instincts had told her to speak to Aristocles directly. She did not want him to think that she was becoming too friendly with the crew of the *Enterprise;* or that she was trying to conceal anything from him.

"James Kirk insists on leading a team inside the mobile anyway," she continued.

One corner of Aristocles's mouth curled up. "Isn't the exploration of unknowns one of Starfleet's prime directives?" he asked, as if to contradict her.

"Yes. The captain emphasized that. But I believe more data should be gathered before anyone enters the object. I can't overrule Kirk, but he did agree at my insistence to take a Tyrtaean along with the team exploring the mobile."

Aristocles's expression changed; had his eyes not been so cold, she might almost have thought he was smiling.

"You, Myra? Are you going?" He asked the question as if the answer might be a threat to him. He was obviously wary of her distinguishing herself in any way.

She shook her head. "He's taking Wellesley. I'm to give what assistance I can to the science officers aboard."

"I hope the object doesn't prove to be dangerous, then. Given that you think it might be, I'm surprised that you agreed to let young Wellesley go inside." It seemed to her that he was setting the stage for future blame.

Myra said, "The mobile is in our system. We have as much right to explore it as James Kirk and his people."

"And better that Wellesley take the risk than you."

She tensed. "It was more practical—"

"Don't look so offended, Myra. I only meant that, as one of our leaders, you shouldn't needlessly expose yourself to danger. I'm sure Wellesley will be most cooperative with the Starfleet personnel exploring that object. A lot of people noticed how friendly he was to them while they were in Callinus."

"It was appropriate to be friendly," she said, annoyed at how he seemed to be searching for benefit from every possibility. "We had to work together. Wellesley—"

"I'm only telling you what some are saying," Aristocles murmured. He looked down for a moment, and she saw that he was cleaning and polishing some eating utensils. Myra suddenly felt conscious of her empty, idle hands. "Besides," he continued, "better to have Tyrtaeans aboard the *Enterprise* who can get along with Kirk and his crew. Having overtly hostile people there wouldn't be practical, now would it?"

Myra said, "We're wasting time, Aristocles."

"Not at all. I think you need to be reminded of where your duty lies." Aristocles leaned forward. "If the alien object can be exploited by us, then it's your job to stake a claim. If it poses any kind of a threat to our world, that threat must be averted. That's your only purpose in being there—to ensure our interests."

She lifted a brow. To keep your interests safe, to

keep your options open, she thought, but said, "We may also learn something, Aristocles."

"If what we learn doesn't serve us, then it isn't of much use."

"We can't know if it's useful unless we first find out what—"

His mouth twisted. For a moment it seemed that he would mock her.

"Useful is not the same as right," she continued.

"Right? Are you serious? You'd betray our interests for what is right?"

She did not answer.

"You don't fool me, Myra," Aristocles said. "You've been curious about that object ever since we found out about it. If it had no practical use at all, you'd still want to study it." And that makes you useless, he did not say.

He had never spoken so frankly to her before, and she knew why he was saying such things now, why he did not even try to hide his true feelings about her. He no longer had anything to gain by trying to smooth over their differences; maybe being openly hostile to her now was to his advantage. He would just as quickly revert to being friendly, if it suited him. The temporary loss of her world's data base had weakened her politically, and Aristocles was ready to exploit any mistakes she made while aboard the *Enterprise*.

And, she admitted to herself, he was right about her curiosity, her impractical desire to learn about things that might be of no use. Perhaps her parents, who were a bit more fanciful than most Tyrtaeans, should have discouraged her theoretical pursuits more, but they had seen no harm in letting her spend hours with her telescope and astronomy books as long as she did her lessons and chores. She had hidden the part of her that dreamed and wondered, but knew that others sometimes glimpsed it; often she had thought that her more fanciful side might be responsible for her political success. Perhaps others sensed the part of her that tried to look beyond her world, and recognized the same suppressed impulse in themselves. Maybe they understood, on some level, that to repress one's imagination was to cripple oneself; surely that was an imprudent and ultimately impractical thing to do.

"Better think of your people," Aristocles went on. "You have to keep our interests uppermost in your thoughts. I worry that so much exposure to representatives of the Federation may cloud your thinking. Just because we and the captain are human doesn't mean that our interests are the same. We're not Earth folk—we're Tyrtaeans. Remember that."

"You're insulting me," she said.

"I'm warning you."

You are trying to demoralize me, she thought. He wanted her to be off guard, to make mistakes; it would strengthen his position. He spoke of Tyrtaean interests while thinking only of his own. Much as she disagreed with his desire for a new and independent Tyrtaean colony, she had once believed in his sincerity; but after nearly two years of working with him, of trying to govern their world together, she had glimpsed his true purpose. He wanted a society in which nothing from outside could impinge on his own thoughts, beliefs, and desires. He wanted a world that would be entirely his own creation, whose people would owe everything to him.

Maybe if she had seen what he was sooner, she could have found ways to work against him, but he now had the advantage. Myra recalled how shocked she had been when Wellesley first told her of the rumors being spread by Aristocles's aides: that she indulged in secret luxuries, that she spent public funds carelessly, even that she was secretly a Federation social engineer. To spread falsehoods was against Tyrtaean ideals; she could not believe that people would waste time in such gossip. She had not known how to fight back.

"I am thinking of our interests, Aristocles," she said, feeling tired suddenly. "Nothing outweighs that in my mind. To have you lecture me on what I already know is wasting time. If I don't sleep now, I won't be able to function as well later, and I'm sure you have other duties. Coles out."

She blanked the screen before he could respond with more debate about the opposition of right to interests; she would have that satisfaction at least. Then she remembered how precarious her situation was, what the penalties would be if she made any grave errors. Exile, they called it, when a Tyrtaean committed a grave offense against society; it might as well be death. She must not make any mistakes that might become weapons in the hands of Aristocles Marcelli.

77

Chapter Five

SULU KNEW FROM the start that he was not going to like it. As he materialized inside the alien worldlet, feelings of unease and distrust slid through him. There was no great sense of alarm. The unease was more like what he felt when a faulty turbolift came to an abrupt stop; the distrust was vague, a whispered warning from an unknown enemy.

A jagged tunnel with black walls was his first sight of the interior. He and the team were inside a tunnel that abruptly turned at ninety degrees into a claustrophobic triangular space. He found the dead-end space annoying, and also disturbing.

Next to him, Janice Rand muttered something about nightmares and solid geometry. Up ahead, Spock was scanning the tunnel with his tricorder. Ensign Tekakwitha stood next to Captain Kirk, looking around with a slightly glassy look in her dark eyes.

It was obvious to Sulu that these passages had not been made for any kind of humanoid life. They seemed to be connections between insect nests.

"Insects," Wellesley Warren said, voicing the same conclusion. "I just hope they're not spiders." He shivered.

Coming from such a tall man, the comment seemed out of place; Sulu had always unconsciously imagined that tall men were rarely afraid of anything. He knew better now, but the old habit of childhood, of imagining that the taller adults around him faced the world fearlessly, rushed back to him in moments of stress.

"You mean giant spiders?" Sulu asked. "I hope not, either."

"Even small ones give me the creeps," Warren said. "I remember when I first told my mother how afraid I was of spiders—it was a long time before I could admit it. She told me that I'd hidden my fear very well, but that the practical thing to do was to proclaim it openly."

"Why was that practical?" Rand asked.

"If people around me know of the phobia, they can handle that easily enough—by keeping spiders out of the room, or compensating for my lapses if my fear makes it temporarily harder for me to function. But if they don't know, they can't do a thing about it in time, and I end up being less useful than I might have been. I might even cause harm."

"That is logical," Spock said.

"I had a great-great-grandfather," Kirk said, "who had a serious problem with spiders on his ranch back on Earth." Sulu noticed the playful look on the captain's face. "The spiders pretty nearly ate him and his horses, after they finished off the local cattle."

"Thank you," Warren said, "for that vivid image."

"We'll beam you back, if you like," Kirk said.

"I'll stay," the Tyrtaean said, forcing a smile. "Don't worry, Captain Kirk. I try not to let my phobia get in the way of what I have to do. Ask Myra about the hairy spiders that overran our camp in the Euniss Mountains once. I managed to kill my share without flinching—and those were Tyrtaean spiders that make Earth's tarantulas look tiny."

Spock was peering at his tricorder. "I think we should go in that direction," he said, motioning to his right.

Kirk nodded. "Lead the way," he ordered.

Spock moved ahead, with Sulu just behind him. As he disappeared around another ninety-degree turn, Sulu hurried after him and nearly collided with the Vulcan. Far ahead of them, there seemed to be a bright green exit.

"What is it?" Kirk called from behind Sulu.

"A kind of phosphorescence," Spock answered in his usual unimpressed way. "I see no apparent danger."

Spock went on, and Sulu followed. "This seems to be an entryway," the Vulcan called out, "to a much larger space." Spock passed through the passage. Sulu stepped out after him—

—into a vast hollow space that made him catch his breath. He stood still in wonder. Here, the green glow was more subdued, but that made it difficult to judge distances. Sulu estimated that the space might be a few kilometers wide. As his eyes adjusted, he saw that black pathways wound across the green expanse in no discernible pattern. This is worse than any maze, he thought; the more he stared at the pathways, the more disoriented he felt. Behind him, he could hear Kirk reporting his observations to Uhura.

"—a wide green space," the captain was saying, "about six—" His voice seemed to fade in and out, and Sulu realized that he could not pay attention to what Kirk was saying. For some reason, the chaotic pattern of the pathways across the green area disturbed him at a very deep level, almost as if something was reaching into him and leaving a residue that would never be cleared away.

He turned away and closed his eyes in an effort to regain his self-control, telling himself that there was no obvious danger. When he opened his eyes again, Kirk was still holding his communicator.

"Kirk out," the captain said as he flipped it shut. "Myra just came to the bridge," he said to Warren. "Uhura will make sure that she hears my report."

"Thank you, Captain." Wellesley Warren looked very pale, his lips black; Sulu knew that it was the light. Janice Rand's eyes were moving from side to side, as if she was expecting something to creep up on her. Tekakwitha stood stiffly, her eyes wide. Only Spock seemed unaffected by the color saturation of the site.

"Shall we continue, Captain?" Spock asked.

Sulu suddenly longed for the captain to order a return to the *Enterprise*. Beam us out of here, his inner voice shouted, and for a moment he feared that he had said the words aloud. He wanted to lie down and cover his head with his arms, but forced himself to keep standing. Warren looked even paler now, but there was a look of determination in his eyes; Sulu felt encouraged by the Tyrtaean's display of steadfastness. His black, tightly closed lips seemed in character.

Kirk shuddered. "It's as if . . ." he started to say, then paused. ". . . as if something's trying to frighten us away," he finished. "What do you think, Spock?"

"I would say, judging from your visible reactions, that some kind of chemical signal may be causing your disturbances. It is unlikely that the mere sight of this interior could provoke them. We also cannot conclude that there is a deliberate attempt here to frighten us off—it may be a coincidence."

Maybe, Sulu thought, remembering what McCoy had suggested on the bridge, this could be the first stage of an alien disease. He pushed the fear aside.

"Ensign Tekakwitha, what do you feel?" Kirk asked.

The young woman took a deep breath. "I feel as if the surface under our feet might suddenly open and expel us into space."

"What about you, Lieutenant Sulu?"

Sulu swallowed hard, then managed to say, "It's more like an extreme uneasiness that could turn into panic. I want to crawl down on the floor and cover my head."

"That's exactly how I feel," Kirk said. "Yeoman Rand?"

"The same, Captain," Janice Rand replied.

"I feel more like Cathe Tekakwitha," Warren said, "almost as if I'm about to fall into space."

"Curious," Spock said, "that your reactions should differ from those of the others."

"Wellesley and I share one characteristic," Tekakwitha said. "We're not as open and demonstrative as the rest of you—excepting Mister Spock, of course. We tend to restrain ourselves. Maybe that predisposes us to have different reactions."

"Interesting," Spock said, then continued scanning with his tricorder. "Still indicating life-forms aboard, but they are registering more weakly. That could mean that they are losing strength." Spock's voice sounded a bit strained; Sulu wondered if by now even the Vulcan was feeling uneasy from the assault of strangeness.

"Steady," Kirk said, as if talking to himself.

"Captain," Spock continued, "we must now consider the possibility that we may not have enough time, given this worldlet's continuous acceleration, to find its inhabitants and to be of any use to them before they perish in this system's sun."

"How long before that happens?" Sulu asked.

"Given the present rate of acceleration, it is a matter of a week or so."

"Where are the life-form signs coming from?" Kirk asked.

"All of them are registering from the other side of this hollow green space." Sulu watched as Spock turned to gaze into the vast hollow once more, but could not bring himself to do the same. "All of the black pathways seem to end up there." He pointed to a distant black spot on the other side of the hollow; Sulu had the illusion that Spock's pointing finger was touching the spot.

Kirk flipped open his communicator. "Kirk to *Enterprise.*"

"Uhura here," the lieutenant's voice responded.

"We'll be exploring in here a while longer," Kirk said. "I'll decide what course of action to take after that."

"Yes, sir. Myra Coles is now with the science officers on the bridge. I'll let you know immediately if their sensor scans indicate any changes in the object."

"Kirk out."

As Spock led the way along one of the green paths, Sulu noticed the deathly silence of the green hollow. The strange glowing light made the placement of the black pathways seem even more haphazard. Sulu felt panic wash over him again; he glanced toward Rand and saw beads of sweat on the ends of her damp, blonde bangs. The pathways zigzagged and turned at right angles, as if doubling back.

Tekakwitha let out a sound that might have been a whimper; then Sulu heard her curse.

"Even spiders," Warren said in a high, toneless voice, "would be better than this."

Sulu felt that the Tyrtaean was simply trying to fill the eerie, sickening silence with words. Spock was still moving forward. Sulu kept his eyes focused on the Vulcan's back.

Only Spock seemed unaffected by the windless, breathless unease of the alien environment, but Sulu suspected that was only the facade of the commander's discipline. The Vulcan's human heritage was deeper than Spock's self-control would allow him to reveal, most of the time.

Sulu sniffed at the thick but odorless air, and imagined that they were moving across a black tendon connecting living muscles of some kind. Finally, in the green haze ahead, another opening appeared: a black wound in a green liver. He made an effort to control his fancy, but it refused to obey him.

They passed through the opening. Spock took another tricorder scan, then motioned to the others to keep moving. An irregular passageway led them past a series of bizarrely shaped chambers. Along the walls were irregular openings from which shone a livid, yellow light. Sulu peered inside each chamber as he passed it and saw strange configurations of corners and walls, all without a single curve or right angle, all apparently designed by an architect who was fanatically devoted to obtuse and acute angles and jagged edges. And somehow, Sulu told himself as his stomach lurched, this designer knew exactly how to sicken him.

Spock stopped in front of one chamber, glanced down at his tricorder, then stepped inside. Sulu went in after him, followed by the others. This chamber's low ceiling was studded with small pyramids, pentagons, and indiscernible solid shapes. Sulu felt almost as if he were inside the belly of a starfish.

Spock said, "None of these interiors seems to have any obvious function."

"How do each of you feel right now?" Kirk asked.

"Dizzy," Warren said.

"I'm dizzy, too," Rand murmured, letting out a deep breath. "Also extremely nauseated."

Gorge rose in Sulu's throat; he swallowed hard. He thought of the ailing crewmembers in McCoy's sickbay and wondered if they had felt as sick as he did now.

"Feel like I'm spinning," Tekakwitha said.

"Same here." Sulu forced the words out. Suddenly he was imagining that the black and green colors would soon impress themselves permanently into his field of vision.

"And I'm not feeling too good myself," Kirk said. "I want all of us to sit down and close our eyes and not to move. That's an order."

Sulu sat down, drew up his legs, and closed his eyes, waiting for his nausea to pass.

Spock, eyes still closed, listened to the breathing of his companions. Their inhalations had slowed, becoming deeper and more regular, so perhaps the worst of their symptoms had abated. He had not felt the dizziness of which the others had complained, but he did feel a tightness in his neck and back, along with a vague uneasiness. Those symptoms had not abated; it was possible that they might grow worse.

"I'm feeling a little better," Kirk said. "How about the rest of you?"

"Better," Warren's voice said.

"I could probably stand up now without losing my lunch," Sulu said.

"Everyone, up slowly," Kirk said.

Spock opened his eyes and stood up, then helped Ensign Tekakwitha to her feet. "I'm all right," she said, but her coppery skin still looked sallow. He let go of her arm, then took out his tricorder and studied what it had caught for a few moments. There was no doubt about it; now that he had a chance to look at the readings more closely, a pattern of sorts could be discerned.

"Captain," Spock said, "my tricorder readings now show something of a pattern. Once it has established a direction that will lead us to the life-forms, and we follow it, that direction abruptly changes. Now the direction to those life-forms seems to lie behind us, across the area we have already explored."

"Odd," Kirk said.

Wellesley Warren moved closer to Spock. "Maybe a protective mechanism is at work," the Tyrtaean said, "one that's meant to misdirect intruders."

Spock was intrigued by the speculative comment. "Why would such a mechanism be needed?" he asked.

"Perhaps because the life-forms are in some way incapacitated," Warren replied, "at least for now. After all, this worldlet seems to have become operational again only recently."

"That's been my suspicion for a while now," Kirk said. "Everything seems to point to their inability to function properly."

"I think we may be assuming too much," Tekak-witha said. "We have no direct evidence for any misdirecting mechanism. There may be something else, something automatic, that's causing our tri-corders to read life-forms where there are none. Thinking they might be hiding, that they're incapacitated—we're attributing motivations to something that may be much more alien than we realize." She waved an arm. "Look at this alien architecture! No humanoid could dream up any-thing like this!" Her skin looked even more yellow, and she was swaying slightly from side to side.

"Unless they deliberately want humanoid life forms to become uneasy," Warren said, "so they won't stay. Maybe humanoids are a type they find especially threatening. Maybe—"

"We don't have time to settle the issue," Kirk said, "or to find out anything about them, before their world goes into the sun."

"Surely they must be aware of their problem by now," Rand said.

"If they're not, in fact, completely incapaci-tated," Warren added. "If they're here at all, for that matter. This may be an empty shell."

"Maybe they know they're headed directly into the sun," Kirk said, "and simply don't care."

Spock considered the implications of that state-ment, that the alien life-forms might be bent upon self-destruction, then turned his attention to the present problem. "The question now," he said, "is whether we are all sufficiently recovered to continue exploration." They all looked unsteady to him.

"Spock, how are you holding up?" Kirk asked.

He looked up from his tricorder. "Adequately, Captain. However, it appears that my reaction time has decreased slightly, and there is an increase in the tightness of the muscles in my shoulders and my neck. The tricorder readings do suggest that something is dampening our synaptic reactions." But he reminded himself that if this were true, it would make all their speculations and conjectures doubly suspect; yet the dampening itself would nevertheless support the suspicion of a mental assault. It was circular reasoning, something he always avoided, but in this case, as in others, he had found that suspicions were not to be discounted.

"Spock, we need more data," the captain said. "Since you seem less affected than the rest of us, I want you to gather what data you can. After that, I think we had all better leave, since it seems unlikely that we'll find either the life-forms or the control center in time to divert the mobile's course."

"Yes, Captain." Spock gazed at his tricorder again. It would be a pity if the chance to learn more about this mobile and its alien creators were lost.

Lieutenant Commander Scott was in engineering, having left Uhura in charge of the bridge. He had intended to run a few standard maintenance checks, having not had much opportunity to check the system over thoroughly while on the surface of Tyrtaeus II. Nothing very important in the checks he and his crew were running; they were the equivalent of polishing the surface of a beloved shuttlecraft, a routine task that had to be done from time to time, for the welfare of the caretaker's soul if nothing else.

Lieutenant Tristram Lund came and stood next to him; the blond man pressed his fingers to one panel. "Everything's working just fine," Lund said.

"Aye, laddie," Scotty said, having expected no less of his engines. "Might as well do some more sensor scans of that asteroid, then. The science officers can always use more data."

It had not escaped Scott from the start that the mobile possessed an advanced drive system that somehow did not reveal more than the impulse principle—not yet, anyway. He was curious to see if he could discover whether it had any interstellar capacity, or was merely a relativistic vessel.

Suddenly his instruments were showing him that the mobile's drive system was capable of something more. Scotty peered at the readings, glanced at the nearest viewscreen, then gazed at his instruments again.

"Will you look at that," Lieutenant Lund muttered at Scotty's right, but the chief engineer had seen what the instruments were telling him even before he spoke. The mobile's drive system was suddenly casting a powerful field around the asteroid, a field more powerful than any use he could imagine for such a vehicle. As he started to scan the field's structure, it abruptly winked off.

"Well," Scotty said, "it doesn't need that much protection for space travel." He hit his console's communicator panel. "Engineering to bridge. Were you scanning that alien thing just now?"

"We saw it," Uhura's voice replied.

"Massoud here," Ali Massoud said. "That field might come up again. It might be a good idea to get that landing party out of there, and fast."

"Just what I was thinking," Scotty replied. "Uhura, open an emergency hailing frequency to the captain."

"Done, Mr. Scott."

"Enterprise to Captain Kirk. Captain!"

"Kirk here." The captain's voice seemed faint.

"Scott here. I'd advise all of you to beam out right away. A strong field of some kind just went on and off around that alien thingee, without any warning at all. It might trap you inside if it comes on again. Did you notice anything from in there?"

"Nothing," Kirk replied. "We can't accomplish anything more here, anyway. Preparing to beam aboard. Kirk out."

Scotty turned back to his instruments, watching to make sure that the team was beamed back safely. He held his breath, afraid that the field might wink on again. Something about the way it had come on and off had reminded him of automatic equipment being tested, as if the alien vessel was preparing for some important action.

"Survey team aboard," the voice of Kyle announced over the intercom, but Scotty already knew that from his instruments. He stared at the sensor readings, wondering what the alien might do now, but the field failed to come on again. He shook his head in puzzlement.

"Lund," he said to the lieutenant, "take charge here. I'm going up to the bridge."

Kirk was sitting in his chair when Scott reached the bridge. Spock was with Ali Massoud and Myra Coles, reviewing the sensor scan records; Wellesley Warren and Cathe Tekakwitha stood with Uhura. Lieutenant Riley had remained on duty as navigator, while Sulu and Rand were conferring with the captain.

"Captain," Scotty said as he came up to Kirk's station, "that thingee out there seems determined to head right into the sun. Did you find anything inside that might help prevent it?"

Kirk shook his head. "Nothing. We couldn't have stayed there much longer. It was too— disorienting."

"To put it mildly," Sulu added. "Amazing how much better we started to feel as soon as we were back aboard."

"Permission to speak, Captain," Myra Coles

said. Scotty turned toward the woman, noting that she continued to adhere to Starfleet form of address, although she seemed to resent the formality. Bonny lass that she was, she could also be as prickly as a patch of briars. She was used to being a leader, he supposed, and it had to be hard for her to bow to someone else's authority.

"Permission granted," Kirk replied, sounding annoyed.

Coles said, "What especially worries me now is that if that field comes on again as strongly as we measured it, and the alien asteroid does strike the sun, the field-effect might either diminish or increase our star's output."

Scotty nodded grimly. "I've been thinking the same thing."

"It might not affect it for long," Coles went on, "but it could be long enough for the people of my world to face some very unpleasant climatic changes."

"What do you think of that, Mr. Spock?" Kirk asked.

"I agree with Miss Coles. I recommend that the object be diverted from its course right away, when it will not take much of an angle to divert it. Trying to do so even several hours from now will present many more difficulties."

"But we don't know what we're dealing with," Janice Rand objected.

"Quite right, Yeoman Rand," Spock said,

"which makes it all the more imperative that we start doing what we can immediately, so that we can determine what we will be permitted to do."

"Permitted?" Myra Coles asked.

"Aye, permitted," Scotty responded. "Lassie, we're dealing with intelligence that won't show itself."

She gave him an annoyed look.

"And also with systems that appear savvy enough," Sulu added, "to deal with our efforts."

"Spock?" Kirk said.

"We will learn more by seeing what we can do," the Vulcan said. "And, given the possible effect that the alien worldlet might have on this system's star, we should act immediately."

Kirk stood up. "Well then, let's take a direct approach, by strapping impulse boosters on the outside of the asteroid and changing its course."

"Aye," Scotty said. "Just what I was about to recommend."

"And once we've diverted it," Kirk continued, "we can spend more time investigating it."

"Let's consider what is going on here," Myra Coles said, moving away from Ali Massoud and closer to Wellesley Warren. "We were to investigate this object. Now we have to divert it from its course." She glanced at the other Tyrtaean for moral support. "Captain, is it possible that you might have caused this problem by disturbing the alien artifact?"

"Wait, now," Scotty cut in, "that's hardly fair, lassie. We all wanted to explore that thing." She gave him another hostile look.

"The unknown always has risks," Sulu said.

"And I must remind you," Kirk said, "that you and Aristocles Marcelli insisted that Tyrtaeans be part of this investigation, not to direct it."

Coles's gray eyes flashed. "Yes, Captain. But I also advised against going inside the worldlet. How do you know that your entering it didn't somehow cause that field to come on? Your actions might be partly responsible for the danger of the field-effect to our sun."

"Myra," Warren said in a low voice, "accusations aren't going to do us any good now. That field might have come on anyway." She shot an angry look at her aide. He continued, "If you'd seen how strange it was inside, how alien—" He paused. "I wonder if anything we've done has affected it, if we can actually affect it at all."

Kirk held up a hand. "I have ordered that we divert the object, Miss Coles. Do you have an alternative course of action to recommend?"

She was silent for a few moments. Scotty felt the tension on the bridge. The captain was keeping himself admirably calm, all things considered, but he would expect no less of Jim Kirk.

"Perhaps," Myra Coles said at last, "we should all just go away and leave this thing alone."

"In the hope that it will stop whatever it's doing?" Kirk's voice was sharper this time.

"That would hardly seem the wisest course of action," Spock added gently.

"If it does stop then, if it does change course, it'll prove I was right. If there's intelligence there, it won't go into the sun. It will save itself."

Kirk said, "And if it doesn't, we'll lose all chance of investigating it further, as well as risking its field coming on again and possibly affecting your sun." He drew his brows together. "You've offered your opinion, Miss Coles. I choose to reject your advice. I am now going to plan the details of how to divert the worldlet with Lieutenant Commander Scott and Commander Spock. Remain here with Mr. Massoud if you like, doing what you can to assist him, or go to your quarters if you prefer. But do not interfere with my orders, or I will be forced to confine you to quarters and then return you to your planet—and that will delay us even more. Time is growing short."

Myra Coles's face paled. Scotty expected her to storm off the bridge. He almost hoped that she would; then the captain could proceed without any more of her meddling.

"Captain," Warren said then, "we've all been under pressure. I think we all have legitimate fears about the asteroid, whether we're willing to admit to them or not."

Kirk gazed directly at Coles. "I meant what I said," he murmured. "You agreed to accept my authority when you came aboard. Either make yourself useful here or return to your quarters."

She lowered her eyes, having the grace to look chagrined. "I'll remain on the bridge for now," she murmured. "I'm sorry, Captain. I won't interfere."

Kirk said, "Now, let's get down to deciding exactly how to keep that thing from immolating itself."

That was more like it, Scotty thought with relief.

Chapter Six

KIRK LEANED FORWARD and watched the shuttlecraft on the bridge viewscreen approaching the alien asteroid. The craft was on automatic; it came close and released one impulse booster pack. The cylindrical pack, ten meters long, propelled itself toward the pitted rocky surface. When it was parallel and six meters away, two harpoons suddenly shot out from the cylinder and embedded themselves in the crust; then the impulse booster reeled itself in until it was resting against the surface.

"So far, so good," Kirk heard Sulu say. The helmsman was back at his station, sitting at the left of Lieutenant Riley.

"Engineering to bridge," Scott's voice said over the communicator. "We're ready for a one-degree deflection from the asteroid's present course. Routine, Captain."

"Very good, Scotty." Kirk sat back in his chair. Myra Coles and Wellesley Warren stood at his right, both staring intently at the screen.

"Once the worldlet is moving in a harmless orbit around the sun," Kirk said, "we can explore it in our own good time."

"All of us?" Myra Coles asked. "Or only Starfleet personnel?"

Kirk took a breath, refusing to rise to the bait. In spite of the courses he had taken in diplomacy, it was getting increasingly harder to control his exasperation with the woman. In irritating situations like this, it sometimes helped him to pretend he was Spock.

"I agreed earlier that you should help us explore this object," Kirk said slowly. "I see no reason to change my mind now unless you impede us in some manner." He paused. "At any rate, if all goes well, you and your people will be free to explore the object at leisure. My crew and I may have a chance only to scratch the surface, so to speak."

"You'd learn enough to tell us whether further exploration is of any practical use," Myra Coles murmured, "and if it isn't, we may not ever be given a chance to mount our own expedition. Some may think it a waste of our resources." A look of regret passed over her face.

"We're ready, Captain," Scotty said from engineering.

"Proceed," Kirk ordered.

Everyone on the bridge was silent as the impulse booster gave its brief push. It was over in an instant, with little to see on the screen. A very small change in the object's velocity, either slowing or increasing its speed, would be enough to change its orbit into a wide swing around the sun. Odd, Kirk thought, sensing the tension in the silence; it was as if everyone on the bridge were expecting something to go wrong. He felt that way himself, and wondered why. Maybe he and the others who had gone inside the alien asteroid had not yet recovered from the disorienting experience.

"Solar orbit achieved," Spock said from his station.

"Very good," Kirk said. Time to relieve the personnel now on duty; Rand, Sulu, and Tekakwitha would be especially in need of rest. He could use some rest himself.

"Captain," Spock said then, "the object is returning to its previous course."

"Aye," Scotty confirmed from engineering. "It's just put a brake on our push with its . . . whatever it is. I don't understand its field drive at all!"

Kirk slowly rose to his feet. He thought of how sluggish he had felt inside the worldlet, and that a thing this alien might never be affected by the efforts of human beings. "Trigger the impulse booster again, Scotty," he commanded.

"Impulse booster exerting its force," Scotty's voice said.

"It's moving into a safe orbit again," Ali Massoud murmured. "Wait a second—what's going on?"

"The alien is resisting," Spock said. "And it is returning to its original heading . . . and still accelerating."

Myra Coles turned toward Kirk. "If you can't divert it," she said in a low but hard voice, "you'll have to destroy it."

He gazed into her angry gray eyes. She was afraid for her world—he could see that in her face—but the political part of her mind was probably already weighing possible courses of action. If the worldlet continued toward the sun, if its mysterious field did perturb the star and consequently altered her planet's climate, the Tyrtaeans—those who survived—would probably blame the Federation, perhaps with reason. It would be on record that Myra had objected to entering the alien worldlet, and Kirk would have no way of proving that his actions had not precipitated the outcome. A court-martial would be called. Even if the Starfleet officers judging him found his actions to have been reasonable, the Federation would need a scapegoat—especially if any climatic changes made Tyrtaeus II far more inhospitable.

He did not even want to think about the possibility, however remote, that the Federation colony might have to be evacuated. The mere threat of that would probably be enough to bring more Tyrtaeans, perhaps most of them, into the anti-

Federationist ranks. Even Myra Coles and her aide might come to believe that their trust in Starfleet and the Federation had been misplaced. Evacuation to another planet could easily convince them to sever their ties for good.

"We still have time," Kirk said, "to consider other options. Mr. Spock, how soon will it strike the sun?"

"Assuming that its acceleration remains constant," the Vulcan replied, "in three days' time."

"Then destroy it now," the Tyrtaean woman said, "while there *is* still time."

"I've made my decision, Miss Coles. We will wait a bit longer."

"It would be a pity to lose this artifact," Spock said, "without making further attempts to divert it into a safe orbit."

Myra Coles spun around to face the science officer. "You tried diverting the asteroid." Her voice had risen to a higher pitch. "It didn't work. It isn't going to work. Only a fool—"

Spock calmly raised one hand and said, "I advise against any precipitous action, Miss Coles."

"It would be the safest course."

"True," Spock said, "in a general sense, but akin to killing the patient to cure the disease. There is also this to consider. If we destroy the object, we lose not only the chance to learn about it, but may also precipitate other events over which we have no control. This mobile is clearly the product of an entirely alien civilization. Therefore, we have no way of knowing what its destruction might bring about. And the attempt may fail, with unforeseen consequences."

"Nothing outweighs the potential danger to my world!" Myra Coles shouted.

"Agreed," Spock said, stepping toward her. "Be assured that we will not deny ourselves the opportunity of destroying the object, if it proves necessary. Self-defense—in this case protecting your world—must take precedence."

"But what will you do before destruction becomes necessary?" Warren asked. "Keep trying to divert it and hope that will work? It might. Maybe we just haven't been persistent enough."

Kirk saw the resentment in Myra's eyes as her aide spoke, as if she thought that even Warren was siding against her.

"We can keep trying," Scotty's voice said over the communicator.

"I have another suggestion," Spock said. "Since I was the least affected of those who were inside the alien mobile, I propose to return to it and attempt to locate a control area. Only a change in an inner directive can alter the mobile's course, short of destroying it."

"And what if you fail?" Myra Coles asked.

Spock was silent.

"Then we will destroy it," Kirk said.

The Tyrtaean woman glared at him. "If you still have time, Captain."

"There's something else," Scott's voice said. "We could lose Mister Spock if we canna' transport him back to the *Enterprise* through that thing's intermittent field."

"You're right, Scotty." Kirk frowned. "Spock, we won't beam you in. You'll go in a shuttlecraft, so you'll be able to get out later on."

"I had already concluded that, Captain."

"But where are the entry points?" Scotty asked. "They're not exactly standing up and announcing their presence. I canna' say how long—"

"Find one," Kirk said firmly, "and fast."

"Aye, be certain I will," the engineer replied. As always, Scotty was overly fond of stressing difficulties he did not really believe in.

Myra Coles sighed, then turned her back to Kirk. Warren glanced at him and shook his head slightly, as if apologizing to Kirk for her behavior. Spock was already heading toward the lift. Everything the Vulcan had said had been eminently reasonable, but Kirk knew that Spock had an additional motive for returning to the mobile, for trying to postpone its destruction for as long as possible: the alien object was highly advanced, representing knowledge that should not be lost to the Federation. And to Spock, personally, such knowledge was as flame to a moth.

Kirk did not object to Spock's motives, and never expected to, as long as all competing interests dovetailed, as they now clearly did. Spock always made sure of that. Exploring the unknown was a Federation directive, but it did not say "at all costs," especially not at the cost of Spock's life.

"Spock," Kirk said, "I want you back here on my order."

"Yes, Captain."

Kirk nearly smiled at the formality, to which Spock always paid precise obedience; but he also knew that his friend would do as he wished, with great care, of course, and that he would not underestimate the danger—even if he, like Kirk, stretched regulations to the breaking point.

Chapter Seven

THE ASTEROID SWELLED as the shuttlecraft approached. Inside the craft, Spock noted the position of the entrance on his display panel. The lock was midway on the long axis of the artifact, in agreement with Lieutenant Commander Scott's coordinates, set down after a complete scan of the alien.

As the shuttlecraft came in on automatic, Spock prepared himself anew to enter the alien. He had restrained his inner turmoil well during the first exploration of the mobile's interior. The lurid green and black environment with its eerily designed walkways had affected the mental states of his companions, but had left his Vulcan mind relatively untouched. His Vulcan physique had also been resistant to the dizziness and disorientation that had so disturbed his fellow officers. But he knew that part of him—his human half, presumably—had been affected by the alien artifact, perhaps deeply. His imaginative capacities, with which his reason had always struggled, had been stimulated and brought to greater wakefulness. The black pathways that seemed to have been designed for insects of some kind had set his suggestible inner vision to conjuring up images of loathsome insectlike creatures, even in the absence of evidence that insectoid beings had constructed the mobile.

Yes, it was logical for him to return to the mobile alone. It was also reasonable to do whatever possible to save the mobile from destruction. Still, his most private self had been unwilling to speak to his compatriots about why he felt such a strong impulse to return alone.

He had wanted to confront it privately, without the distraction presented by companions. Now, alone in the shuttlecraft, he again faced his need for an exclusive audience with the alien, and once more found it surprising that he should have such an impulse and be so willing to obey it. He again put it down to his human half.

His desires were irrelevant, Spock told himself as the shuttlecraft attached itself to the place that seemed to mark an entrance. The need to divert the mobile from collision with the sun was paramount, outweighing any of his inner motivations.

The helmet of his protective suit was equipped with both a display readout from his emergency subspace transmitter backpack and a tricorder readout from the portable case hanging on his shoulder. As he rose from his seat, determined to find the mobile's control center, he again considered the plan that he and Lieutenant Commander Scott had devised. Once the shuttle was attached, and waiting as a means of ultimate retreat, he would search the alien interior in sections, dividing it into six roughly equal parts. As he completed a search of each section, Scott, now stationed in the transporter room with Lieutenant Kyle, would lock on and bring him to another section. This would save some time; there was no way he could search the vast interior on foot.

As his shuttlecraft lock opened, Spock found himself facing an indented, flat, rocky surface that had all the appearance of an air lock. Scott had not had an easy time finding it; the task had taken three scans and some analysis of the data. The possible entryway was closed.

Spock reached for the tricorder that hung from his shoulder. "Mr. Scott," he said.

"Scott here."

"I may not be able to get inside from here. I am scanning the mechanism right now, and there seems to be no obvious way to trigger it to open. It may be that it will open only to identification patterns of some sort, ones that I am not equipped to provide."

"Try a series of different frequencies," Scott said. "That might do it."

Spock thumbed the tricorder, running from low pitches to high frequencies even his Vulcan ears could not hear. "I have done so, but they are ineffective."

"Spock," Captain Kirk's voice broke in, "we don't have time to try cracking an alien safe combination. Have Scotty beam you inside from your position."

"Captain," Spock said, "I remind you that I may not be able to beam out if the mobile's field comes on."

"I'm well aware of that," Kirk said, and Spock heard the concern in the captain's voice.

"If it becomes necessary for me to make a hasty exit from the mobile, I would then have to try to open this lock from the inside, with my phaser, if need be."

The captain was silent for a moment. "You could use your phaser now, and leave yourself with a ready-made way out—but we don't know what such an action might trigger. Don't do it."

"I agree that it is unwise to do damage to the mobile now, Captain. It is possible that its systems may interpret such an action as an attack. We would be wise to wait until there is no other choice. Beam me inside, Mr. Scott."

"Do it, Scotty," Kirk added.

The flat, metallic surface of the mobile's air lock faded from Spock's eyes for a moment, and was replaced by the green and black alien interior. He scanned the area with his tricorder, and again his scan suggested life-forms somewhere nearby. It seemed to him suddenly that there were a great many of them, whispering in an incomprehensibly alien language, preparing to hunt his thoughts.

"I am here," he said aloud. If they could not understand his words, perhaps they could somehow sense the warning in his mind. "There is an approaching danger from which you must save yourselves. Your vessel is traveling rapidly toward this system's sun, and we have been unable to alter its course. You must act very soon, or you will perish."

The whispering grew louder in his mind, as if insects were invading his brain. He felt almost as if tiny creatures were crawling around the inside of his skull.

Then, suddenly, the whispering stopped, as if a great wave had broken on some inward shore and slipped back into the deep. His tricorder readings still indicated that there were life-forms nearby.

Spock moved forward through a jagged passageway, wondering what waited for him.

"Spock," Kirk said at his station, "report."

"Still no sign of any kind of control center, Captain," the Vulcan's voice replied. "I am beginning to think that it may not have one, as we understand it."

Myra Coles and Wellesley Warren had come

back on the bridge shortly after Sulu and Riley had returned to duty at their stations. The Tyrtaeans might have rested in their quarters for a longer time, since they weren't really needed here; but they would be thinking of their world's safety.

"Speculations, Mr. Spock?" Kirk said.

"I surmise that control may be exerted over this vessel by mental means, perhaps originating in various centers of mentality, possibly a mixture of both artificial and biologically rooted intelligences, linking to power capacitors."

"Interesting," Cathe Tekakwitha said. She sat at the library and computer station, where she was now on duty with Ali Massoud.

"That might explain," Spock's voice continued, "why I'm picking up life-forms, always nearby but never seen. Perhaps they are everywhere, extended throughout the structure. It might also explain why we experienced so much psychological unease."

"Do you mean that they might have been trying to contact us?" Tekakwitha asked.

"Quite possibly."

"Or that they were deliberately trying to scare us off?" Kirk said.

"That is another possibility," Spock replied.

Myra Coles sighed. "But then our only hope for diverting their mobile is to get them to do it. And if they fail . . ."

"Yes," Kirk said, accepting the conclusion. "Then we may have to destroy it."

"Mister Scott," Spock said, "transport me to the coordinates for the second sector."

"Aye," Scott's voice replied from the transporter room. "Here you go!"

"He must not give up too soon," Wellesley Warren was murmuring to Myra Coles. "Spock still has five sectors to search."

"Mr. Spock," Kirk said, "what do you see now?"

"More erratic passageways and the same green and black color configuration."

Kirk frowned at the sound of his first officer's voice. Maybe he was imagining it, but was it possible that Spock's voice sounded awed, even humbled? Perhaps the artifact was slowing the Vulcan's mind.

"Captain," Myra Coles said, "this is getting us nowhere. You should get him out of there and decide if this thing is going to be destroyed."

He turned toward her. "As a last resort, Miss Coles, as a last resort. We'll continue to keep pace with it as it moves toward the sun, and destroy it only when we have to."

She pressed her lips together. "Do you think this is easy for me, insisting on its destruction? Destruction is waste, and we Tyrtaeans hate waste."

Kirk stood up slowly. "I said that I would act when necessary."

"The time is now, Captain Kirk. Take no chance at all. Bring Commander Spock back and destroy it now while you still can."

"Miss Coles has a point, Captain," Spock said. "Only our scientific curiosity prevents action. But I still concur with you that curiosity must override caution for now."

"We may be destroying intelligent life," Kirk said as he sat down again. "More to the point, if you insist on being practical, we may destroy something that could retaliate for our action. That could mean a much worse problem than a possible climatic change for the people of your world."

"I did say earlier," Spock murmured, "that we might set in motion an unforeseen chain of events, but I am somewhat doubtful that one such event would be retaliation. The life aboard this mobile has taken what seem to be defensive measures, but has not moved aggressively against us. This may be an egoless artificial intelligence, standing outside ethical judgments."

"I appreciate your dispassionate observations, Commander Spock," Myra Coles said. She turned to Kirk. "With something that alien, you may be taking more risks than you realize by waiting. Bring him back now and destroy the thing."

"Mr. Spock still has time to search more of the interior," Kirk said as calmly as he could. "I prefer to stick with that plan for now."

"I am in agreement with you, Captain," Spock said, "but in the meantime, you might try the impulse booster again."

Myra Coles's gray eyes narrowed, and her

thoughts were clear: You Starfleet officers all stick together.

"Mr. Scott," Kirk said, "try the booster again."

"Aye, Captain. Scott to engineering—fire booster."

"Activating now," said the voice of Lieutenant Lund.

It might work this time, Kirk told himself. Maybe they just hadn't been persistent enough, and this time there would be no resistance from the alien mobile; in which case, the problem would be solved in the simplest way: the asteroid would continue in a sun orbit and could be explored at leisure.

Myra Coles was gazing at the viewscreen, and he saw his own look of hope in her eyes.

"Course corrected," Lund said from engineering. "Projection shows a free and clear sun orbit, cometary."

"Confirmed," Massoud said from his station on the bridge.

"Now let's see if it sticks," Sulu said softly.

Kirk waited; everyone on the bridge was silent.

"No luck," Lund said over the communicator. "It's corrected its course toward the sun again."

"Confirmed," the computer said.

"That thing wants the fire!" Scotty's voice shouted. "I can feel it."

"Did you hear all of that, Spock?" Kirk asked.

"Yes, Captain."

"What do you suggest now?"

"I propose to leave after six more hours. That should give me at least enough time to explore the remaining sectors in a cursory manner. I do not wish to fail without at least trying to collect as much data as possible. Is that satisfactory, Captain?"

"Proceed, Mr. Spock," Kirk said softly.

Myra Coles shook her head. "Captain," she said, "please consider that something could happen within the next six hours that could keep you from doing anything with the mobile. It may be able to defend itself. It's my world we're talking about, and your first officer's safety."

"Miss Coles, my first officer is capable of assessing risks, and I trust his judgment." In spite of his words, Kirk's reason was telling him that Myra Coles was right, that destroying the object would be the safest course. Starfleet would no doubt commend him for putting the welfare of the Tyrtaeus II colony ahead of other considerations; Myra Coles would be able to send a message to the Federation Council saying that she and Kirk had been entirely in agreement. Maybe the Tyrtaeans would even feel some gratitude to Starfleet for protecting them from possible danger, and there would be less talk of a new colony and breaking away from the Federation. Apart from all of that, Spock would be safely back aboard ship.

But, without saying it, Spock was telling him to wait; he seemed determined to explore the mobile for as long as possible. Thoughts teased him: the mobile had been hiding in the cometary ring of this solar system; perhaps it was not the only such mobile; there might be others. He shook off his suspicions—no point in making matters worse by inventing more threats.

Kirk stood up. Myra Coles was watching him intently. "I think we may have given this thing all we can," he said.

Wellesley Warren looked dubious. "So you are going to destroy it?" Kirk could hear the disapproval in his voice.

"One step at a time," Kirk said, "but it looks as though we may have to." I'll know when the time comes to destroy it, he told himself, because all his instincts insisted that it wasn't time yet. There will be time, he told himself, to do what has to be done.

Chapter Eight

"CHRISTINE," Leonard McCoy said to Nurse Chapel, "you take charge here. I'm going to the bridge."

Christine Chapel nodded. "I hate to say it," she said, "but I agree with Myra Coles. I hope the captain can get Spock out of there."

McCoy left sickbay and hurried down the corridor toward the lift. With the recovering crew members ready to return to duty, and no medical emergencies requiring his attention, he wasn't needed in sickbay for the moment. He had been listening to the exchanges over the intercom as he worked. Jim Kirk sounded as though he hadn't gotten enough rest, and that Coles woman surely wasn't making things any easier for him. Neither was Spock. McCoy couldn't tell which of the two annoyed him more, Myra Coles for sniping at Jim about problems he was already well aware of, or that blasted Vulcan for insisting on unnecessary further exploration of the mobile.

McCoy sighed as he entered the lift. In all fairness to Spock, he thought, Jim was probably just as curious about the alien as Spock was. He admitted to himself that he was growing more intrigued by the thing. Even Myra Coles probably wanted to learn more about the mobile, but her duty to her people would outweigh any curiosity she felt.

The captain was standing by the library and computer station, conferring with Ali Massoud and Cathe Tekakwitha, as McCoy came onto the bridge. Myra Coles and young Wellesley Warren stood near Uhura.

The Tyrtaean woman glanced at McCoy. "Greetings," she said, and he could hear the irritation and weariness in her voice.

McCoy inclined his head to her. Warren smiled tentatively at him; Coles frowned.

"The captain has already acknowledged that he's probably going to have to destroy that thing." Myra Coles waved a hand at the viewscreen image of the asteroid. "But he insists on postponing any action against it for as long as possible."

"I've been listening in, ma'am," McCoy said, drawling the words slightly.

Kirk left the science station and returned to his post, nodding at McCoy as he passed him.

"Mr. Sulu," Kirk said as he sat down, "set a

course to parallel the mobile's path into the sun, and prepare a spread of photon torpedoes to strike in four quadrants and dead center, but upon my order only."

"Aye, aye, Captain."

"Mr. Spock?" Kirk said.

"Yes, Captain," the Vulcan's voice replied. "We must be prepared for all eventualities."

Myra Coles asked, "So why haven't you beamed your first officer out of there?"

The low pitch and extremely measured tones of Kirk's voice told McCoy that Jim was working hard to contain his annoyance. "Be assured that I will risk neither my first officer nor your world, if the danger is clear."

"Will you risk a developing world on your hunch?" Myra Coles asked. "Even the smallest danger is too much to risk. We can't just wait and see what happens when our sun swallows this thing."

"Miss Coles," Kirk said, still in the same measured voice, "I'm well aware of what it means to weigh possibilities. If I make a mistake, you and your people won't be the only ones affected. My ship and my command are also at risk, as they are with all my most important decisions. I could lose both my command and the *Enterprise* if Starfleet finds my judgment here mistaken."

Maybe that will shut her up, McCoy thought. In spite of himself, he felt some sympathy for Coles;

reason was on her side, even if she wasn't helping the situation much by hectoring the captain.

"I see," she said, "but—"

"I'm well aware," the captain continued, raising his voice slightly, "that the population of a planet can't be risked in favor of an unknown. I have no more time to discuss this, Miss Coles. If you don't shut up and keep out of my way, you will be escorted from the bridge and restricted to your quarters."

Myra Coles paled. The sudden look on her face was one of outrage, but she was silent.

"Captain," Spock's voice said then, "I will be finished exploring this second sector soon, and if I do not find a control center or another way to divert the mobile from its course, we should let nothing stand in the way of the Tyrtaean colony's safety."

Well, McCoy thought with some surprise, Spock and he were actually in complete accord.

"Then we are all agreed, Captain?" Myra Coles said, sounding more subdued.

"Mr. Scott," Kirk said.

"Aye, Captain."

"Beam Spock out as soon as he gives you the word. Mr. Spock—can we conclude with certainty that the collision of this unknown with the star will produce adverse effects on Tyrtaeus II?"

"We cannot know that with absolute certainty," Spock replied. "We do know that the mobile does possess an advanced field-effect drive system, one that may affect stellar bodies. Perhaps it will not affect them in a way that would put a planetary environment at risk, but we cannot be certain of that. A star is massive enough to swallow and obliterate just about anything without being affected."

"Certainty isn't the point," Myra Coles muttered, so softly that McCoy could barely hear her. "This risk doesn't have to be taken. It *shouldn't* be taken."

"When you're finished with that sector, Spock," Kirk said, "I can give you four more hours."

"Six hours are what we agreed upon earlier," the Vulcan's voice murmured, "and almost two have passed." McCoy saw the look in Coles's gray eyes and knew what she was thinking—that even that time was too much.

"Four hours," Kirk said, "and out you come. Mister Scott, return to engineering and monitor developments from there. Mister Kyle, beam Commander Spock out when it's time."

Kirk gazed at the viewscreen for a while, then looked up as McCoy approached his command station. The physician had a conspiratorial look on his face. McCoy glanced aft at Myra Coles, then said in a whisper, "I could probably dream up a reason for getting her off the bridge for a while. Another medical scan, maybe—after all, the stress of space travel—"

"Don't bother, Bones." Kirk preferred to have Myra there; she could snipe at him all she liked as long as she did not interfere with anything crucial. He did not want her to think that he was making decisions behind her back; he would not give her a chance to claim later that he had treated her unfairly, ignored her advice, or had not properly considered the interests of her people. She deserved some consideration for that. She had put her trust in the Federation, and had been its advocate on her world. He would have to do his best not to betray that larger trust.

"Captain!" Tristram Lund shouted from engineering. "The asteroid's thrown up its field again."

"Confirmed," Ali Massoud said from his station aft. "Sensor display here shows the same thing."

"Let me see that, laddie," Scott's voice said over the communicator. Kirk waited, knowing what the chief engineer would tell him. "It's true," Scotty continued. "The field's up, and we canna' transport anything through it without grave risk. The field density readings are very clear about that. They exceed all safeties!"

"Spock, did you hear that?" Kirk asked. "Come out physically, through the lock."

There was no reply.

"Spock! Can you hear me?"

"The channel is still open, Captain," Uhura said.

"Spock!"

"Spock here."

"Can you hear me?" Kirk asked.

"Yes," Spock responded. "My communicator link was cut off, but the field does not seem to affect my suit's subspace channel."

"The field is still up, Mr. Spock," Scott said. "You'll have to get out of there on your own."

Kirk gripped the arms of his chair. "Spock, can you find your way back to the shuttle?"

"Yes, Captain. I read its position clearly."

"Leave now. That's an order." He waited for Myra Coles to say something. Mercifully, she was silent.

"Captain," Massoud called out from his station. Almost simultaneously, Kirk heard Scott's voice on the intercom.

"Go ahead, Scotty," Kirk said.

"The worldlet's acceleration is increasing," the engineer said. "We're losing even more time, Captain."

Kirk's fingers tightened on his armrests. Next to him, McCoy cursed softly. He could almost hear what Myra Coles was thinking, what she would say at any moment now. You'll let it go into the sun, Captain, rather than kill one of your officers. You'll put Spock's life above that of my world. What will you do if he can't get out in time? Will you destroy the mobile then? You should have listened to me, you should have brought him out. . . .

It was all taking on an air of inevitability, he thought. One by one, the doors to reasonable choices were closing.

Who was it, he found himself wondering, that had said, "Life must be lived forward, but understood backwards." He had a better way to put it: "Fate is what you see looking back. Looking ahead, you don't see as much."

Well, he told himself, he was looking ahead, and he still had some moves left to make.

Uhura turned in her seat and looked up at Myra Coles. The Tyrtaean woman was standing stiffly, hands clasped, watching the viewscreen with empty gray eyes that seemed to be expecting the worst. Uhura saw that she had finally realized how grave the situation was, that there was nothing she could say now that would change anything for the better. Myra had at last understood the dilemma Captain Kirk and his first officer faced, that was now theirs alone to solve—if they could.

Myra moved closer to her aide. "Exile," Uhura heard the woman say in an undertone to Wellesley. "That's what this may mean. I'm one of our leaders—people will be much harder on me, much quicker to pass sentence. I know I shouldn't care about that now, but I do."

Exile, Uhura thought. She recalled her last day in Callinus, when Wellesley and two of the more friendly Tyrtaeans had invited her and Cathe Tekakwitha to dine with them. The food was plain, as always, but the other people in the tavern had been friendly—by Tyrtaean standards. Wellesley's two comrades had requested a song from her, and then the talk had turned to the civil order that predominated in Tyrtaean life.

"I must compliment you on that," Tekakwitha had said. "This has to be one of the safest places in the galaxy. As far as I can tell, you have almost no crime at all, even without any prisons or police."

"What would be the point?" Wellesley responded. "No Tyrtaean would want to show anyone that he wants something so much he'd steal it. There's little to steal anyway. Rape, murder, assault—they all grow out of impulses we work hard to control. Most of us also live in small towns and settlements, where we can observe what's going on. We all make sure that our dwellings and work places are secure, and we all know how to defend ourselves."

"Fact is," one of his friends added, "we can be our own police. No one's going to depend on somebody else to get him out of trouble. And the penalty for serious offenses is something no sane person would risk."

Uhura was curious. "And what is that?" she asked.

"Exile to the northern continent," Wellesley said, averting his eyes. "No one survives it." He had clearly not wanted to say much more, and Uhura, after checking some records later, had wondered why there was no mention of the punishment in the Tyrtaean chronicles.

The Tyrtaean leader glanced at Wellesley, took a step toward the lift, then stopped and stood very still. It seemed that she was not going to leave the bridge after all. Uhura turned back to her console. Myra would remain there, she knew, a witness to events, ready to give her version of what had passed afterward.

"What if Spock can't get out in time?" Myra murmured. Uhura turned toward her again. "What then? Will James actually destroy the mobile with him on board?"

"You heard what he said," Uhura replied. "The captain will do whatever he has to do."

Myra Coles took a breath. "When this is over, James will not be able to say what suits him. I made my protests. They will be on record. There will be two of us to tell the truth." The woman sounded as though she was already preparing her own defense.

"Spock," the captain's voice said inside his helmet, "the asteroid's acceleration is still steadily increasing."

"Understood, Captain." Spock, moving through an irregular black corridor, still could not accept that the alien mobile was without an accessible control area. His reason kept insisting that finding such a facility would present the simplest solution to the mobile's sunward plunge. Otherwise, he would have to conclude that the vessel was out of control, with no intelligence in command except decaying systems; or that the mobile's life-forms were intent on self-destruction, that they in fact wished to collide with the sun.

Suicides, Spock thought, are usually beyond thinking of what might happen to anyone around them.

"Are you on your way to the shuttlecraft?" Kirk asked.

"I will make my way there presently." Spock glanced at his tricorder reading. "The reading for life-forms is now stronger than ever, Captain. Moving ahead for a look."

He went slowly up the jagged black passageway. He was sure that his perceptions had been affected by the alien construct; several times, when he had been in the more open areas of the mobile, he had reached out with his hands toward a jagged pyramid or strange green shape, thinking that it was within reach, only to discover that it lay far beyond his grasp. Once he had come up against a wall that he had not been able to see clearly in the intensity of black and green. He was losing his sense of perspective.

Suddenly he realized that he was lost in this corridor.

"Spock," Kirk said more insistently, "the rate of acceleration is continuing to increase. There is no longer time left for exploration. Get out now."

"Yes, Captain." He hurried forward and made one turn, then another. The corridor grew tighter. He seemed to be having more trouble breathing, and imagined the walls suddenly closing in on him and crushing him; that was part of the sensation that human beings called claustrophobia. A third bend in the hallway brought him into a narrowing that he could not push through; his shoulders caught between the walls. He saw a way through up ahead, but he could not reach it even if he took off his protective suit.

Farther up the corridor there was life, registering clearly on his tricorder display, without revealing what sort of life it might be. It frustrated him to think that a control area for the mobile might be just ahead, where he might be able to alter the alien vessel's course, and that he could not reach it.

"Mr. Kyle," Spock said, "can you increase power for a moment, lock on, and beam me forward of my present position fifty meters?"

"Negative," Kyle replied. "I wouldn't try to lock on through the field even if I could see your position."

Fifty meters, Spock thought, might make all the difference to save the mobile. Even if he was transported imperfectly, all that would matter would be the completion of the task. One life—

"Is there a chance the field might lift for a moment?" Kirk's voice asked.

"Negative!" Scott shouted from his station. "The field's intensified, and the mobile's rate of acceleration is still increasing. That field is obviously part of its drive system."

"Spock, come out," the captain said. "Get out now."

Spock backed out of the tight passageway. "Heading toward the shuttle now," he said.

It was taking Spock longer than he had expected to get back to the lock where he had left the shuttlecraft. The twisting black pathways and black and green corridors were taking their toll; twice he had taken a wrong turn, even with his tricorder to guide him.

Very well, he told himself; if his vision could not aid him, then he might have better luck by not relying on it.

He closed his eyes, feeling his way along the corridor with his hands. As he moved, the sensations of disorientation and dislocation eased a little. At last he came to a turn that felt oddly familiar, and opened his eyes.

"Captain," Spock said slowly, recognizing the area, "I am now at the air lock."

"You don't have a moment to lose," Kirk replied.

The lock was a flat, ebony surface surrounded by a metallic border of green, irregular in shape, resembling a distorted pentagon. Spock ran his hands along the border, looking for a button or panel, but found nothing. Perhaps the air lock's controls were not physical ones.

"There seems no way to trigger the lock," Spock

said. "Mr. Kyle, can you beam me into the shuttle-craft now?"

"No, Commander Spock."

"That damned field's still up," Scott added wearily, "and it's growing stronger." Spock could not tell if Scott was still in engineering or had returned to the transporter room. "We can't beam you out."

"Use your phaser," Kirk said. "That's an order—you have no choice."

"Yes, Captain." Spock was already reaching for his phaser; he set it to the proper intensity, then aimed it at the doorway. "Firing now."

The beam shot out with its familiar hissing whine of ionization and stood like a bright drill against the black surface—

—without effect.

Spock lowered the phaser for a moment, raised it to the maximum setting, then opened fire again. The beam stood bravely against the alien hull, whining until the power pack drained and died.

"Captain," Spock said, "I cannot cut myself free. My phaser is exhausted."

"And we still canna' beam you out," Scott said with dismay in his voice.

"Stand by," Kirk said, and Spock already knew what the captain had in mind. "Mr. Spock, move back from your position. We're going to recall the shuttle, to get it out of the way, then use the ship's phasers to open the mobile and get you out. We'll send the shuttlecraft back for you after that."

Spock left the entryway and made his way back down the passage.

McCoy was about to say that he had a feeling it wouldn't work, that it would be too easy, that Jim had waited too long, that he should have kept Spock from going into the mobile in the first place. But he kept silent, knowing that any remarks he made now would accomplish exactly nothing.

The alien mobile seemed to be waiting on the screen as the *Enterprise* readied to bore away with its phasers.

"Spock, brace yourself," Kirk said.

"Ready, Captain," Spock replied.

Myra Coles had come forward to stand near McCoy; he saw the doubt and fear in her face.

"He's very trusting," she murmured. "Spock, I mean. It's in his voice. He so obviously believes that James will get him out of there."

He was about to say that she was reading too much into Spock's usual expressionless tone, but restrained himself. "I suppose he does," McCoy said at last. It was nothing new.

"And James won't let him die."

McCoy was silent. He knew that the captain would make the right decision if Tyrtaeus II was in danger; he would not risk imperiling millions of lives for Spock's sake. But, as usual, Jim would do everything he could to find another way, to bend the rules. He'd blackmail God or the Devil if he had to, McCoy thought, to get his own way; it was the kind of persistence that wore away mountains with drops of water.

"Open fire, Mr. Sulu," Kirk ordered.

Sulu's hands moved over his console. "Phasers locked on target, Captain."

The beam reached out across the silence of space and splashed against the alien.

"Cease fire," Kirk said.

"Aye, aye, sir."

The beam winked out, and the screen view pulled in for a closer look. There was no sign of an opening, no sign of any damage.

"Fire again, Sulu," Kirk said, "and hold on target for thirty seconds."

"Yes, sir. Engaging now." The beam shot out and stood against the moving worldlet as the *Enterprise* stood off in its position.

"Captain," Tekakwitha called out from her station aft, "the object's velocity is increasing. It's at half our impulse-power speed right now—it's extraordinary."

"Only six hours from the sun's corona," Massoud added.

"Confirmed," Scott said from engineering.

"Fire again," Kirk commanded, raising his voice. "Hold for two minutes this time."

Again the beam lashed the alien. Myra Coles leaned forward, her eyes wide. McCoy was certain that everyone on the bridge had probably guessed the implications of what they were seeing. If full power from the ship's phasers was having so little effect, then striking with photon torpedoes might not do any better. The alien would not be easily destroyed.

As the beam shut down again, with no effect, Spock said, "You must fire photon torpedoes within the next hour to have any hope of diverting the object's course . . . or of destroying it in time."

The Vulcan might be pronouncing his own death sentence. McCoy lowered his eyes for a moment, wondering if Jim would be capable of acting.

No one on the bridge spoke for a long time. At last Kirk said, "Keep pace and ready the torpedo spread."

I should have known better, McCoy told himself. James Tiberius Kirk would sacrifice Spock, if necessary, to do his duty. What that would do to his innards, McCoy did not want to know, but the captain would meet his responsibility to the people of Tyrtaeus II. He glanced at the Coles woman and saw that her gray eyes were glistening, as if filling with tears at the prospect of what was coming. Reserved as she was, she would still weep for her people—and, he suspected, she would also shed a tear for Spock.

Kirk looked toward McCoy, then back to the viewscreen. "Spock," he said, "we're going to fire the barrage."

"I understand, Captain."

"Fire!" Kirk shouted, almost as if cursing at himself.

The photon torpedoes shot out like swift electric

eels through the black of space, and struck the mobile's rocky surface. McCoy tensed, expecting to see the rocky surface wounded and the mobile pushed off its course.

But the asteroid was still on the screen, seemingly immovable and invulnerable. McCoy heard Kirk's stifled sigh of relief precede his own. Sulu turned for a moment to look at the captain, his face betraying his relief; he would not be Spock's executioner after all.

"Wait!" Massoud shouted from his station. "The torpedoes had some effect after all! We have a course change that will put the mobile into a solar orbit."

"What?" Myra Coles said, clasping her hands tightly in front of her.

Kirk was very still. "Spock, are you there?" he asked after a moment.

"Yes, Captain. I felt some vibration from the torpedoes, but the area around me seems unaffected. Tricorder readings indicate no damage to this section of the mobile."

"Captain." The low-pitched voice over the communicator had the sound of resignation and despair. It was Scotty's voice, and McCoy suddenly knew what the engineer did not want to say. "The damned thing is correcting its course again. Heading back into the sun."

"Oh, no," Myra Coles said softly, "oh, no." Again McCoy wondered if she was thinking of Spock's fate or of what might now happen to her world. He wanted to believe she was thinking of both.

Wellesley Warren came to her side, looking concerned. "It will be so terrible for him," McCoy heard her whisper to her aide, and he wondered if she was speaking of Spock or of the captain.

Kirk got to his feet. "It's not over yet," he said, staring coldly at the screen. McCoy felt the captain's determination move through the bridge like a force of nature.

"But what can you do?" Myra Coles moved past McCoy and toward Kirk. "If the torpedoes couldn't stop it—"

"I was prepared to do what had to be done," Kirk said in a toneless voice, "even if it meant the death of . . . of one of my crew. That ought to convince you that I also had the interests of your people at heart."

"I wasn't thinking of that, James. I never doubted that you did. How I wish . . ." She bowed her head. She would be thinking, McCoy thought, that if Jim had listened to her, he might not now be facing this dilemma. Maybe he had provoked the thing into defending itself by going inside it in the first place. Maybe he should have acted earlier.

"Spock," Kirk asked, "how can the mobile resist phaser fire and photon torpedoes?"

"Unknown, Captain. Its hull would have to be carbon neutronium at the very least, but with mass and inertia completely neutralized, to move as it does. I am speculating, of course."

"Jim," McCoy said then, "you've got to get him out of there. That thing's going into the sun, and nothing can stop it."

"Spock?" Kirk asked. "Any suggestions?"

"The only possibility for changing its course now," Spock answered, "is still to find some controls aboard this vessel."

But there weren't any controls, McCoy thought, realizing that Spock would probably be lost after all. He had been shielded from the photon torpedo barrage, but there was no way that he could survive the hell of the sun.

Chapter Nine

HE HAD FAILED his friend. Kirk knew that he would carry the burden of that knowledge for the rest of his life. Unjustly, for him it would outweigh the bitterness the Tyrtaeans would feel if their world and environment were irretrievably damaged or lost, and the almost inevitable court-martial if that happened. His will remained strong, but he wondered if he would have the heart to defend himself, to make the case that his actions had been justified. He thought of the court-martial that had been instituted against him not long ago, when he had been unjustly accused of causing an *Enterprise* crewman's death. He had thought that might be the end of his career. Spock had saved him that time, by discovering that the starship's computer programming had been altered, and that the crewman, who was working out a grudge against Kirk, was still alive, hiding aboard the starship.

"I am sorry, James."

He turned and looked into Myra Coles's face.

"About Commander Spock," she continued.

"It wouldn't have happened if I'd followed your advice," he said.

"I wasn't going to say that." She looked away. "If our sun is affected, and my world suffers because of that, my people will look for someone to blame. They know that Starfleet will deal with you, but my fate will be in their hands. They'll remember that Aristocles and I insisted that one of us be here to help in exploring the mobile, and that I was here to advise you. Many will remember how I always defended our ties with the Federation. That you didn't listen to me and didn't follow my advice may not be enough to redeem me in their eyes."

Kirk said, "You'll lose the next election, I suppose." He said it as gently as he could.

Wellesley Warren stepped closer to her. "That would be the least of Myra's problems, Captain," the young man said. "When a Tyrtaean commits a grave offense against society—and, believe me, it happens rarely—the punishment is exile."

"Exile?" Kirk asked.

Warren looked uncomfortable. "The accused is tried in a public place before a jury of sixteen Tyrtaeans." He spoke in a monotone. "He must make his own case and speak in his own defense. Anyone who wishes may come forward to offer evidence, either for or against him. If a majority on the jury votes against him, the offender is taken to our northern continent, where the climate is extremely harsh, and given only a few tools, weapons, and some provisions. Anyone who can survive alone there for five years will have his offense forgiven, and is welcomed back into society. Only one person has ever survived exile." Warren paused for a moment. "You see, we Tyrtaeans are a practical people, and such a punishment is much simpler than building a prison or devising original forms of execution—practical also in that anyone who survives exile has demonstrated his self-reliance, earned forgiveness, and proven his worth to the rest of us."

"There's nothing about such a punishment in your public records," Kirk said.

"Of course not. What would be the point? If the offender is exiled, it's best to forget him. If he lives and is forgiven, why keep a record of his offense? There again, we are practical."

"Some offenders choose not to struggle on," Myra said softly. "There are rumors that several committed suicide in the early months of their exile. Suicide would have been their final act of self-determination."

"Myra," Kirk said softly, and put his hand on her shoulder for a moment, but he could not speak.

Spock would perish and the solar output might be affected. Even a tractor beam at full power would not be able to stop an object accelerating to well beyond two hundred kilometers per second. The best that could be hoped for would be that the star would swallow the alien artifact and there would be no further consequences. He would escape his court-martial and Myra would not be punished by exile. She would still lose much—the next election for sure, and perhaps also the debate with those who wanted to found an independent Tyrtaean colony, but at least she would have her life; and all he would lose was whatever knowledge the mobile might have yielded, and his closest comrade.

No, Kirk told himself, I refuse to accept even that.

He sat down at his station again. "Spock, can you hear me?"

"Yes, Captain."

"Tell me what you think of this wild supposition. If this thing can resist photon torpedoes and phaser fire, and is made of the kind of materials we think it is, is it possible that it could resist this sun's interior?"

"Perhaps, Captain. But this vessel's interior will reach extreme temperatures unless there are systems in place of which we know nothing as yet. I doubt that I could survive even if the object maintains its integrity for a time. At best, if it could resist heat and pressure indefinitely, I would still be trapped inside without provisions and little prospect of escape."

"Yes, of course," Kirk said, feeling the hopelessness creep back into him once more. He was useless; he could do nothing; there was nothing to be done. No, he told himself. To admit defeat now would only ensure that he lost in the end.

"I will attempt one more stratagem," Spock said, "in the time I have left. I propose to go back to the narrowing passage without my utility suit and attempt to push through to the forward section of the mobile. There is still a slight chance of finding controls there and altering the alien vessel's course."

"Do it, then." Any course of action was preferable to doing nothing at all. "In the meantime," Kirk continued, "we'll give the mobile another shove with our impulse booster. It's worth a try. Scotty, do you hear me?"

"Aye, Captain. Ready to do it now."

The people on the bridge were silent, waiting through long minutes as the booster gave the mobile its invisible push.

"It's not working," Scotty said at last. "The object is still correcting its course for the sun."

Kirk said, "Then try to pull it off course with our tractor beam."

"That might change its course slightly, but the same thing will happen. It'll just return to its present course, and we'll only drain our power."

"Mr. Scott is correct," Spock said.

"Do it anyway," Kirk said. "That's an order, Scotty."

"Readying now," Scotty said.

Kirk looked around the bridge. Both Janice Rand and Tonia Barrows were coming out of the lift. The two yeomen would be concerned for Spock, but Kirk guessed that wasn't the only reason they had come to the bridge together. They would also be wondering how their captain was holding up under the strain. Yeoman Barrows hurried to McCoy's side; Yeoman Rand moved to Kirk's right.

"Tractor beam locking on," Scotty announced.

"Confirmed," Sulu said.

"Pull back at half," Kirk ordered.

He saw no change on the screen. The alien remained a silent affront.

"Pull at full," Kirk said.

"Pulling at full," Sulu replied.

"No luck," Scotty called out from engineering. "It keeps resisting."

"Continue," Kirk said, glancing at McCoy. The expression on the doctor's face was one of compassion, for a colleague who was trying in vain to raise the dead.

"Maintaining at maximum," Sulu replied.

"It just won't budge!" Scotty shouted.

"Exceed safeties," Kirk ordered. "Put as much power as possible into the tractor."

"Aye, sir," Scotty said.

"Exceeding," Sulu answered.

"Hold," Kirk commanded. "Scotty, can we get another tractor on it?"

"Not on this short notice, Captain!"

"Then give it all the power we have."

After a moment, the lights on the bridge went out, and the emergencies came on.

"No luck," Scotty said. "And even if we could move it off course, it will only correct."

"Release," Kirk said, then sat back.

The main lights came on as the emergencies winked out.

"Jim, are you all right?" McCoy asked.

Kirk nodded at him, then at Yeoman Rand. "I'm fine," he said, trying to sound as though he meant it.

"It's astonishing!" Scotty cried from engineering. "That thing insists on heading for the hellfire!"

Kirk heard the anguish and frustration in Scotty's voice. The frustration was that of an engineer who could not get his way. The anguish was for Spock.

Spock took off his utility suit, then removed his backpack and portable equipment from it. After attaching his communicator and now-useless phaser to his belt and slipping his tricorder case over his shoulder, he picked up the backpack and made his way again to the place where the life-form readings had been strongest. It was logical to conclude that somewhere on this mobile some intelligence was attempting to avoid the coming catastrophe.

He came to the narrowing of the passageway and began to squeeze through to the turn. He pushed through, careful not to become wedged between the walls, then took his communicator from his belt, set the channel to tie into the subspace communicator core backpack, and flipped it open. The communicator should have enough range to work through the backpack, which he would leave here.

"Captain," Spock said, "I have reached an open right hand turn, and am going forward." The walls of the narrow passageway were slippery, almost wet, and felt as though they might either close on him or suddenly give way. "The walls have an odd texture to them, but that may make it easier for me to pass through."

"Noted," Kirk responded. "Spock, we're . . ." The captain was silent.

"Captain?"

"We're going to have to change course within two hours."

"I understand. Spock out."

He squeezed through the passage, then checked the temperature reading with his tricorder, expecting to see a slight rise, but there was nothing. Close enough to the sun, this green and black interior would become a geometrical inferno. His Vulcan physiology made him able to tolerate fairly high temperatures by human standards, but beyond his own limits he would surely die. When the mobile entered the sun, he would be far beyond all limits.

He moved through the corridor slowly. Ahead, he saw a strange glow—odd because there seemed to be a tinge of blue in the green. He narrowed his eyes, studying the slightly different color of the glow until he was sure that what he saw was not an illusion. He closed his eyes and felt his way along the passageway, and suddenly sensed that he was nearing—what?

Spock opened his eyes. He stood in front of an open, oval entrance. Quickly, he took more readings with his tricorder. Life-forms—and the readings were stronger than ever.

He stepped inside and found himself in a dome-like interior. He turned, looking around the chamber, then took measurements with his tricorder. Although the circumference of the floor looked circular, it was actually an oval, and near its center a heptagonal panel jutted from the floor's black surface.

As he approached, his tricorder readings told him that it was four meters high and a half-meter thick. Light streaked across its surface. This, according to his tricorder, was the source of the life-form readings.

The lights flickered and darted like ghostly fish through a solid ocean, and Spock hypothesized that, to one degree or another, they might be capable of motion through the solid material of the mobile. That would account for some of the tricorder's earlier readings. The life-forms inside the heptagonal wall might be the remains of the mobile's artificial intelligences; or perhaps they were what was left of the builders themselves, who had translated themselves into their artifact.

It occurred to Spock at that moment that the alien forms might be living in a kind of subjectively eternal hell, trapped in their suffering for eons, but had finally been able to steer their container, their ancient instrumentality, toward the release of death. Perhaps their creators had abandoned them, left them to evolve fortuitously into a greater, more painful awareness. The *Enterprise*, he realized again, might very well be engaged in a struggle with an alien bent on suicide.

Kirk sat at his command station, considering what else to attempt, then got to his feet and turned aft. "Massoud," he said to the science officer, "would it be possible to punch a hole in that field and beam Spock out?"

Massoud replied, "Picking up a material object and maintaining its integrity through such a field is a formidable problem. He'd be scrambled, at best."

"I wager we'd lose the subject completely," Scotty added from engineering. "We canna' take the chance."

"How about trying with something inanimate," Kirk said, "just to give us an idea of what's possible."

"Aye," Scotty responded, "we could try that."

"We must try everything," Kirk insisted. Myra Coles was staring fixedly at him; Yeoman Barrows moved closer to the Tyrtaean woman, as if preparing to restrain her. But Myra would not give vent to her feelings now; the situation seemed to have finally defeated her, as it might soon defeat them all.

"Send Spock an extra phaser," Kirk said. "He might need it."

"Phaser ready to be beamed to the mobile," Kyle said from the transporter room. "Locking on."

"Kirk to Spock," Kirk said. "We're sending you a present."

"I will remain at this position until I receive it, Captain," Spock replied.

Kirk caught the eye of Wellesley Warren; the young man gazed back with sympathy. Kirk imagined what lay ahead: the loss of Spock, changes in the solar output caused by the alien mobile, he and Myra Coles engaged in their dance of accusation and counter-accusation when a court-martial hearing was called. She would have to argue that he and the *Enterprise* crew should have left the mobile alone, that they had thoughtlessly triggered responses in the alien unknown, that he had ignored her advice. And she would be right, up to a point, knowing that she would have to make such arguments before her people in order to have any chance of saving herself.

But exploring the unknown, especially alien artifacts, was a standing Starfleet order. And it might turn out that Tyrtaeus II would be unaffected by the alien's plunge into the sun.

He sat down at his station. "Kirk to Spock."

"Spock here."

"Did you get what we sent you?"

"Yes, Captain, and the phaser appears to be intact."

"Mr. Scott, listen carefully." Kirk took a breath. "As a last resort, could we risk beaming Spock out, at full power and scanning resolution?"

"I wouldn't do that," Scotty said. "It's too risky."

"But he'll die anyway if he's left there."

"True, Captain," Spock said. "I believe that we are now at the point where almost any action or inaction is likely to lead to my demise." He was silent for a moment. "I must report that the phaser you beamed in to me is devoid of its charge. Coming through the heavy field around this mobile has apparently drained it."

"Then that's that," Scotty muttered.

"Spock," Kirk continued, "do you want us to try to beam you out at the last minute?"

Moments passed with no answer.

"It will be your decision," Kirk added. A knot twisted inside him.

"Negative, Captain. At best, I would be stored as scrambled or incomplete information in the transporter, with almost no chance of regaining coherence."

"Good God, man!" McCoy burst out. "Do you prefer a certain death?"

"A nearly certain death, Doctor." Spock's voice

seemed a bit fainter. "There is still a chance—a very small one, to be sure, but a chance—that I can find some sort of control panel."

"Captain," Scotty cut in, "the mobile's field density is increasing, and its acceleration is increasing by a factor of five each second."

"Spock?" Kirk said. "Spock? Can you hear me?" There was no answer, and he knew what Scotty's next words would be.

"The field's cut off the subspace link, Captain," the chief engineer continued, "and the mobile is leaving us behind. We're at full impulse now. It'll hit the sun in less than half an hour."

Spock stood before the alien panel, studying his tricorder readings. By now, the sun would be very near, and yet the temperature inside the mobile remained steady. He knew that as the mobile entered the sun, it would begin to ablate material from its outer surface, until the inner shells were reached. Heat would be expected to increase at any time now, until everything inside was incinerated. The asteroid would burst like a kernel of popcorn and be dispersed as a gas in the upper reaches of the solar atmosphere.

He did not have much time left.

His reason kept insisting that his only hope for survival was in this alien panel, assuming that it was a control center of some kind. But the panel might be a device beyond his power to comprehend, a purely aesthetic artifact, or even a virtual world in which the alien life-forms lived, oblivious to their coming fate.

Spock put his hand against the panel, and suddenly the chamber darkened. An image of the space around the mobile appeared on the inside of the oval surface, covering it completely. Stars shone, and the sun of Tyrtaeus II was near enough now to take up a quarter of the field. The *Enterprise,* hanging nearby like an ornament, still paced the mobile, but he knew that very soon it would have to turn away. These stellar images were all in a dim, black and white monochrome. This was another sign of how unlike humans and Vulcans the builders of this artifact must have been; the display had clearly been built for beings with a very different visual physiology.

Strangely, as the sun ate up the field of view in the oval chamber, his tricorder did not register any change in temperature. He checked the readings often, certain that the tricorder was not malfunctioning, and concluded that this lack of temperature increase had to be caused by a temporary benefit offered by the alien technology. Even if the mobile resisted disintegration for a time as it entered the sun, the buildup of heat inside it would be unstoppable, at least by any cooling system that he knew.

With this artifact's endurance, Spock thought, he might live long enough to see the mobile engulfed—from the inside—as the entire inner viewing surface of the oval chamber became a sheet of seething, falsely cold light.

He continued to gaze at the chamber's starry display. At last he saw the bright bauble that was the *Enterprise* begin to pull back, and he knew that his end was very near. . . .

"Captain," Scotty cried from engineering, "that damned thing is still accelerating, like a spear shooting straight for the sun!"

Kirk did not answer as he searched for a way out of the dilemma, a way out for Spock. The Vulcan had to come out. It was as simple as that: he had to come out. It could be done easily, by simply reaching in through the alien field and grabbing him—mangling him in the process. He would be out: hopelessly damaged but out. Repairable? Kirk asked himself if he dared try it, even if Spock refused.

"Scotty, how close can we go in?"

"A ways still, but what's the point? There's nothing we can do."

Nothing, Kirk thought, except to pull Spock out through a shredder.

"Scotty, can we still transport through that thing's field?"

The engineer did not answer for a few moments.

"Scotty?"

"No, Captain. Nothing can get through now, in any way. It's a wall."

Kirk sat back and took a deep breath. Even that slim hope was gone.

"Pull away, Mister Sulu," Kirk ordered, his voice breaking. "There's nothing more we can do here."

Sulu obeyed the order.

As the *Enterprise* pulled back, the alien mobile seemed to become fixed on the bright disk of the sun, a dark spot becoming smaller with each second.

It became a point, and seemed to hang there for an eternity. Kirk did not have the heart to order further magnification of the object carrying his friend to a blazing death.

The black point winked out.

Janice Rand bowed her head.

"Oh, no," whispered Tonia Barrows. Kirk felt a hand grip his shoulder and knew it was McCoy's. Looking up, Kirk saw that the physician was not only struggling to contain his own feelings, but also worrying about his captain's mental state.

And then the bridge was silent, except for the intermittent beeping of its instruments, and Kirk had the foolish notion that this was the hushed silence before some cosmic surprise party, when all the goodness in the universe would leap out of the darkness and reverse this tragedy. The loss of Spock became even more painful as he tried to imagine the foreboding and fear that would already be preying on the minds of Myra Coles and Wellesley Warren. Whatever now happened to this sun could not be prevented. His mostly diplomatic mission to Tyrtaeus II, so routine in the beginning, had failed in a way that he could not have anticipated; and he would not have Spock at his side to deal with the consequences.

He tried to see ahead to what those might be: the evacuation of a colony; court-martial; the end of his career; an all-too-human bitterness which would be with him for the rest of his life.

Chapter Ten

THE BRIDGE OF the *Enterprise* became a timeless place, silent except for the sounds of instruments like insects. Human will had failed to have its way. This was nothing new, McCoy told himself, seeing into James Kirk's mind and finding there the usual appalled, insulted sensibility that demanded to be exempted, that behaved as though it could never bet on the losing numbers of the wheel. That was what his friend Jim had always wanted, and it was astonishing how often he got his way. He kept his few failures in a dark dungeon below the foundations of his mind, expecting them to die there when merciful memory erased them. But all that McCoy could see now, looking ahead, was a man who might one day be left standing alone, with all that he had known gone, struggling not to care, but caring nonetheless. . . .

Ironically, what had always saved Kirk was his Starfleet training. Combined with his basic temperament, it allowed him to recognize the next best thing in the face of imminent defeat. Even when it was obvious that the game itself could not be changed, he would labor to accomplish the third or fourth best thing. Jim would accept Spock's loss, mourn him, and then deal with the next problem.

Yeoman Barrows glanced at him, as if somehow agreeing with his thoughts, then turned her gaze back to Kirk. She and Janice Rand stood stiffly, their faces tense, their eyes on their captain as they awaited his next order. Blasted Vulcan, McCoy thought, realizing abruptly how much he would miss Spock.

"Mr. Massoud," Kirk said hoarsely, "are there signs of any disturbances in the sun from having swallowed the alien vessel?"

"None, Captain," the science officer replied.

"But it's too early to tell," Scotty's voice said over the intercom.

Kirk did not turn to look in the direction of Myra Coles. McCoy glanced aft and saw the concern in the Tyrtaean woman's eyes.

"Mr. Sulu," Kirk said, "set course for a return to a standard orbit around Tyrtaeus II." His voice was as decisive as McCoy had ever heard it.

"Aye, aye, sir," Sulu responded.

Again, the instruments sang on a silent bridge. Kirk sat back at his command station and closed his eyes for a moment, and it seemed to McCoy that he was searching for Spock within himself.

"Captain!" Uhura called out suddenly. "I'm picking up a subspace signal . . . out of the sun! It seems to be . . . Mr. Spock!"

Kirk sat up as if awakened from a nightmare. McCoy looked toward Uhura. The communications officer was shaking her head, looking as unbelieving as he felt.

"Let's hear it, Lieutenant," Kirk said grimly, as if expecting nothing. Perhaps, McCoy thought, struggling against the hope that was rising inside of him. The message might be nothing more than some kind of delayed signal.

"Spock to *Enterprise*," the Vulcan said, his voice filling the bridge. "Captain, as incredible as it may seem, I am alive and well."

Yeoman Barrows cried out and clutched at McCoy's arm. Behind him, McCoy heard a gasp.

"Spock!" Kirk shouted, leaning forward. "Where are you?"

"I would say, with a high degree of confidence, that I am in what might be called a subspace sun-core station. Is my signal coming from the sun?"

"Yes, it is," Uhura answered.

"Spock, what's happened?" Kirk asked with relief.

"From my observations," Spock replied, "here in what seems to be a control center, the mobile

157

entered the sun through a warp window, which opened, after some difficulty, to receive the mobile. I would say, from what has happened so far, that the mobile knew where it was going."

"But will it stay there?" Kirk asked.

"There seems to be no further activity. For the moment, I plan to stay in this control area, where I expect to be able to gather more information. There is a kind of screen in front of me, which now shows nothing. The life-forms detected earlier seem to be part of the very structure of the mobile, with more intensive readings registering in the instrumentation site—if I may call it that—before which I am standing."

"We have to get you out of there," Kirk said, and McCoy nodded in agreement. The mobile had defied their predictions so far; there was no telling what might happen now.

"I would consider that advisable, Captain," Spock said, "but I doubt that the transporter can cut through both the sun's fields and the subspace barrier. I also do not think that we can call this space, within which the core station is located, subspace as we know it. Perhaps it should more properly be described as a kind of 'otherspace,' congruent with but shielded from the sun's interior state in normal space. Any other configuration would be intolerable to any physical structure. I do not see any obvious immediate danger, but one must ask how long this oasis will sustain itself. It may be quite old and subject to chaotic instabilities."

"You mean that it might fail," McCoy said softly, "and be engulfed by the sun."

"Yes, Doctor."

"Is there anything you might be able to do before then?" Kirk asked.

"I shall attempt to discover how to open the warp window that seems to be the entrance to this station. If I am successful, I suggest that you send in a probe. If it arrives safely, you could then send in a shuttlecraft for me, since I have no other means of exiting."

McCoy was growing impatient and fearful as he listened. The vagueness and generality of the Vulcan's suggestions seemed unequal to the task.

"We'll certainly try that, Spock," Kirk said, and McCoy heard hope in the captain's voice. "We'll get you out."

"I realize," Spock continued, "that such a plan may be unworkable. But before I can act more specifically, I must study the controls in here—if the objects on this wall before me *are* controls. Perhaps one of them commands the entrance to this station."

Or perhaps not, McCoy thought, wanting to wish away his skepticism; he had seen Spock and Kirk confront and overcome too many seemingly insurmountable difficulties in the past to discount their chances of even a partial success. Still, a barrier might rise one day that could not be breached, a knot tighten that could not be loosened, an end come that could not be undone. But not now, he told himself anxiously as he watched the sun on the screen; not yet.

McCoy struggled with his doubts. Jim had spoken to his trapped friend as if summoning Lazarus forth from a tomb of fire and light. But Lazarus had come out by way of a miracle.

The waiting was nearly unbearable, but Kirk refused to count the minutes. He had ordered Sulu and Riley to be prepared to launch a probe toward the sun. He listened as Scotty reported again from engineering. There were, according to Scotty, still no signs of disturbances in the sun; Massoud confirmed the engineer's observations.

That was good news, Kirk told himself, trying to believe it. As long as nothing changed, Spock was still safe.

"Spock to *Enterprise*."

Uhura tensed at her station and adjusted her earpiece with one hand.

Kirk sat down again at his station. "Kirk here."

"Captain, I have been unable to find anything that might be a set of controls."

Kirk tensed. "The probe is ready, Spock. We've set the coordinates to follow the path by which you entered. Shall we send it in?"

"Yes. I now suspect that the warp window opens

automatically to receive any vessels approaching at those coordinates."

"It had better open," Kirk said. "Launch the probe, Mr. Sulu."

"Probe away," Sulu said.

The screen showed a small object whisk away from the ship and lose itself in the glare of the sun. Long before it got close enough to be destroyed, it would enter the coordinate window, Kirk hoped, and penetrate to where Spock was trapped—if the window opened automatically. Doing it was the only way to find out if Spock was right.

"Tracking the probe, Captain," Riley said.

Kirk sat back and waited, trying not to worry about how Spock would escape if the probe met a fiery end and a shuttle could not be sent in to get him.

"It's penetrated the sun's corona," Riley added after a few moments.

"It must be inside," Scotty said over the communicator, "since our sensors show no evidence that it's been destroyed. If it had, by now it would be no more than vapor inside the sun's photosphere, but there's no sign of that."

"But, sir," Massoud said from his station, "isn't it possible that it could have been destroyed beyond the reach of our sensors, somewhere inside?"

"Mr. Spock?" Kirk's hands tightened on the arms of his chair. "Any sign of that probe at your end?"

"Scanning now, Captain." There was a long pause before the Vulcan said, "The probe is registering on my tricorder, in an area just outside the mobile, and it appears to be undamaged."

Kirk felt some of the tension leave his body. "Good. We'll prepare a shuttlecraft to go in unmanned. Board it and get out of there at once."

There was no way to foresee what complications any delay would bring. Maybe the alien portal would close permanently; maybe its mechanism would trap the probe, the shuttlecraft, and the alien mobile for good. Spock might not be able to leave, or might die in the attempt.

"I shall leave as soon as the shuttlecraft arrives," Spock said slowly, "although it would be most interesting to stay and explore a while longer. The interior of this mobile grows more fascinating the longer I am here."

"Is it safe, Mr. Spock?" Uhura asked.

"I see no obvious danger now, Lieutenant."

Kirk drew his brows together. Spock did not sound like himself; he seemed distracted.

"Mr. Spock?" Kirk said firmly.

"Yes, Captain?"

There it was again—that odd bewildered tone that did not sound at all like his Vulcan friend.

"Once you're out," Kirk said, "we can consider going in again, although we can't be sure the window will stay open. Do you have an idea of what keeps it open?"

"Haven't you and Spock pushed your luck enough?" Myra Coles asked.

Kirk was almost relieved to hear the sharp, angry tone in her voice once more. "I take risks, Miss Coles. I do not push my luck. I will get Spock out, and then consider what to do based on what he has discovered."

She sighed. "If the sun actually remains unaffected by that mobile, Captain, we'll be a lot luckier than we deserve to be."

"You heard Miss Coles, Spock," Kirk said. "She has a point. Still, I imagine that Starfleet will want this sun-core station explored if the entryway remains open. Do you see anything inside the mobile that might control it?"

"I am endeavoring to find . . . something . . ."

"Spock, we're launching the shuttlecraft. You have only as much time as it takes to arrive."

Spock had again sounded disoriented. Kirk tapped his fingers on his armrests, then said, "Be ready as soon as it's inside. Board it at once—any more investigation will have to wait until another time. Is that clear?"

There was no answer.

"Spock? Answer me!"

"The channel is wide open," Uhura said. "It's just . . . it's almost as if there's no one at the other end." Her fingers danced across her console. "Mr. Spock. Mr. Spock, can you hear me?"

"Spock!" Kirk shouted, afraid suddenly that his

first officer might have lost consciousness and was lying there, unable to communicate. Perhaps the alien controls had protective mechanisms rigged to injure anyone who tried to manipulate them. He might be severely hurt, or even dead.

"Spock, answer," Kirk said more softly as he stood up. "Spock? Spock!"

He waited for his friend to respond.

"Hold the shuttlecraft," Kirk said at last, sitting down again. "It won't do him any good if he can't get inside."

He considered what to do next.

"Shuttlecraft holding," Scotty said.

The bridge was silent, waiting for his next order.

"Do we send the craft, Captain?" Scotty asked, "or keep holding?"

"No—shut it down," Kirk said.

Chapter Eleven

As Spock faced the alien panel, he sensed that something was attempting to raise him up . . . to what? Knowledge that would forever quiet his curiosity? Another state of being?

Part of his mind advised caution. Spock felt no fear, only uneasiness and an increased awareness of danger far greater than a threat to his life. Yet he could not draw away from the panel. As he placed his hand against it, he felt malleable and suddenly drained of will—

—and he was walking across an empty, red plain beneath a warming, red sun. His equipment was gone, but he was still clothed in his Starfleet uniform. The clothing felt different on his body, as if it did not quite fit. He looked down and saw that his boots had vanished; the red grass was cool underneath his bare feet.

His legs carried him over the countryside. He tried to stop, to turn back, but his body would not obey him, as if he had never been still and his motion was the realization of some deeply repressed wish.

He gazed around at the rolling land, then noticed a black forest to his right; sable-colored leaves that resembled ferns hung from twisted black limbs growing out of cylindrical black trunks. Above the forest, on a hill, sat a strange orange structure of cylinders and walls. At his left, a green river drained into an emerald lake. Somehow, he could also see the lake within himself, even though the quiet, green body of water—or a liquid that resembled water—remained before his eyes.

This, Spock concluded from that clue, was the secret of the alien mobile: it was a support system for a virtual civilization, one that had long ago turned its back on the given physical universe. But it was impossible for that civilization to reject reality completely; so its people had constructed a mobile that would have access to as much energy as the culture would ever need, by drawing it from suns.

As his mind began to search for additional confirmation of his conclusion, Spock saw a group of humanoid shapes emerge from the forest. They came quickly toward him across the red field, violating the familiar laws of motion and perspective; they seemed to be in one place, then appeared suddenly in another much closer to him, with no discernible movement in between. That odd perception seemed further verification of the nature of the artifice that held him. He found himself moving toward the beings in a long, flowing motion that reminded him of both song and dance, in the *largo* style so beloved of his mother, and he wondered why his motion should so differ.

Yet in what seemed only a moment, he was face to face with the alien delegation. He was about to lift one arm in greeting, then hesitated, wondering if they might interpret the gesture as a threat.

The beings were plain, hairless bipeds, with ageless, flat, humanlike faces and large, dark eyes. There were six of them, all near his own height, and he suspected that this was their true appearance, although they might have come to him in any guise. The fact that they had not done so, that they had not appeared to him in a completely alien form, indicated a desire to allay his fears.

What do you want of us?

The unspoken question insisted, without Spock's sensing it in any particular language.

Why did you disturb our life?

Spock frowned. What he was feeling now was similar to the sensations of a mind-meld, but with too many barriers for him to read more than conscious surface thoughts.

It was an accident, he replied silently. Our aim was exploration. We thought at first that this was an abandoned artifact, with no living beings inside, but a scan with our instruments revealed that there were life-forms aboard. We tried to communicate with you, and did not attempt to enter your vehicle until we had failed in those efforts. We feared that you might perish in the sun, and also that your entry into the sun might pose a danger to one of the inhabited planets in this system.

Spock felt them assenting to him. It seemed to him that they understood, that in fact they were rapidly grasping his thoughts and learning his mind as he attempted to convey to them why he was here.

As he waited, Spock was again struck by the alien beauty of the artifice around him. It was a second nature, an inner landscape into which these people had moved. He could not tell if the vista resembled the world of their evolutionary origin or if it was an environment they had imagined. He wondered what they did here, how they lived, how they might gather new knowledge about the outward universe from such an inward perspective. And he concluded that they would not look outside, that they might no longer be interested in anything beyond the reality they had fashioned.

For this, they relied on the mobile's artificial intelligence, Spock realized. As caretaker of their world, its task was to acquire vast amounts of energy to synthesize, out of the mind-stuff of its charges, whatever they might wish. Enormous amounts of information had to be processed to maintain this world of what seemed to be parks of rest and culture, spacious estates set in a mental landscape. The mobile's intelligence, its interface with the universe of origins, was still following its directive—to keep its people alive—and that was why it was here, inside the Tyrtaean sun.

We understand.

That thought seemed to come to Spock from the entire delegation.

Will you be leaving soon? they asked him.

I expect to, Spock replied.

He wondered if the mobile's entrance into the sun involved previously existing stations, set up remotely for this very eventuality, or whether the pocket was set up as needed just before the arrival of the vessel.

There was no answer to his curiosity.

Suddenly he looked up and saw a shadow sweep across half the sky. The group of humanoids swayed slightly, and it seemed to him that they were disturbed by the dark specter. At once their questioning reached into him, as if he had caused the shadow.

What is it you fear? Spock asked.

That shadow is something outside, trying to reach us. Do you know who or what this might be?

You have nothing to fear, Spock responded. My companions are merely searching for me.

And they will not harm us?

There is no reason for them to harm you. Once they understand your . . . way, you will not be disturbed. Spock restrained his thoughts for a moment. He had almost said *plight,* because that was how virtual worlds were regarded in Federation directives, as fantasies in which their dreamers were transfixed.

Plight?

He realized that they had glimpsed the word he had tried to take back.

Plight? the alien minds repeated. We do not regard it so. As long as we have enough energy to live in our creations, to become our creations, we do not look back to our origins. That universe is only one among infinite possibilities, and not to be preferred to one of our own making.

Debatable, Spock thought, but he would not argue the matter. He recalled the Talosians, who had been withering away inside their illusory world. And yet, in an act of mercy, he had taken his former commanding officer, Captain Christopher Pike, to them. On Talos IV, the crippled and physically broken Pike would have the illusion of physical health and strength, as long as he never left the planet. But Spock had also known that such a world was a trap, and that the Federation had been right to forbid its starships ever to travel to Talos IV.

You are kind in what you did for your former superior, but very wrong about us. We differ from the world you remember with so much distrust. We know the difference between dream and reality, between illusion and brute matter—and we have chosen to raise our worlds against the outside . . .

Spock was unable to object as the alien thoughts raced ahead of him.

. . . but we do not neglect our knowledge of the universe that surrounds ours. We see the story in your mind, which proclaims that the book of life is the story of intelligent life's war with nature, the struggle between village and jungle, between city and barren wilderness, between habitat and desert. We have known the given world, and have come to prefer our own. We will not wither and die, but we do demand to be left alone in safety.

I understand, Spock insisted. We adhere to a prime directive, which commands us not to interfere with the development of other societies.

But then Spock's curiosity was roused once more, and he asked:

You said "worlds," in the plural. Are there more of your mobiles in the galaxy?

He felt hesitation, then reluctance, as if someone was trying to shield his/her thoughts. Then the answer came:

As you would say, that is a manner of speaking. Our worlds exist one within the other, growing forever inward as the need arises . . . in the manner of the artifacts called Russian dolls that you have just brought to mind.

Spock had been thinking exactly that, seeing the wooden figures nested inside one another.

Magnificent, he replied. I am most impressed.

Calm flowed through Spock. Do not be concerned, the aliens whispered to him. It is the common weakness of those who give themselves to subduing infinity.

What do you mean? Spock asked.

The infinite, given universe cannot be subdued, or finally understood. It is an insult to the very reason that you so prize, and with which you attempt an endless task. It is better to seek within, and remake what can be remade.

But the outside remains, Spock objected. It stands off, implacable and other.

That may not always be so. . . .

"There's no choice," Kirk said. "We must send in a manned shuttlecraft. If Spock's hurt, he may need help getting aboard."

"I'm willing to go," Wellesley Warren said.

Myra Coles glanced at her aide. "I won't try to stop you, Wellesley," she said, "but I'm certain that the captain will."

"You're right," Kirk admitted. "This is work for Starfleet personnel."

"I volunteer, sir," Sulu said.

"And I'll go, too," Uhura called out from her station. "You might need a communications officer aboard if—"

"No," Kirk replied. "One person in the shuttle is enough." He longed to go himself, but his place was on the *Enterprise*. He had violated standard procedures too often, as Spock had tirelessly pointed out.

"The shuttlecraft is ready, Captain," Scotty said from engineering, "and I'm willing to take her in myself."

McCoy moved closer to Kirk's command station. "May I remind you," the medical officer said, "that the buddy system is always a wise idea. Whoever you send as pilot, someone ought to go with him. Spock may be badly injured and need emergency medical treatment—so I'm the logical choice."

"Christine Chapel would do just as well," Kirk said, "or anyone else on your medical staff. I don't need to send you, Bones."

McCoy leaned over Kirk. "I know what you're thinking, Jim," the physician said in a low voice. "But you and I both know that you'd rest easier if you had me there. Right?" His voice fell to a whisper. "For God's sake, Jim—he's our friend."

Kirk glanced back at Uhura and saw that she had heard. She nodded, and Kirk said, "Very well, Bones. It's you and . . ." He paused. Not Sulu. He knew then what his choice had to be, and caution be damned. "It's you and me."

Myra Coles seemed about to object, but everyone else on the bridge was silent.

As he looked around at their faces, Kirk realized that they all knew it had to be this way. Only those who were closest would risk everything and do their utmost. For a moment Kirk was reminded of trial by combat, the medieval practice according to which the victor was presumed to be innocent because he had the most to lose. Strength flowed from the purest motives, by the gift of divine grace. Yes, we understand, the faces of his crew said. You must go. You have no choice.

"Take care, James," the Tyrtaean woman said at last.

"Sulu, you'll be in command until we get back," Kirk said.

"Aye, aye, sir," Sulu said, and Kirk heard the tone of inevitability in his voice.

"And if McCoy and I don't come back, Scotty will take command of the *Enterprise*."

"Yes, Captain," Sulu managed to say with a semblance of discipline.

Chapter Twelve

THE SHUTTLECRAFT shot out from the *Enterprise* and came around in a wide turn to run at the Tyrtaean sun. Kirk glanced at McCoy and said, "Let's hope that window opens up to let us in without any trouble."

"I should have known that cursed Vulcan would drag me into something as bizarre as this," McCoy mumbled, less to Kirk than to himself.

Kirk shook his head, trying to smile. "I was the one who decided someone had to go in with the shuttlecraft. If you thought I was out of my mind for suggesting it, you could have relieved me of duty."

"I volunteered for this," McCoy said. "So that has to mean I'm as crazy as you are, and not competent enough to relieve anyone of duty."

Kirk watched the sun grow on the viewscreen, filtered and made safe for human eyes. What was it that a classic science fiction writer of the twentieth century—a man named Campbell—had called suns? He tried to recall the phrase: the mightiest machines, cooking up the periodic table of the elements, making all life possible. Yes, a sun was the mightiest machine, an open hearth furnace at the center of its solar system, formed as the stellar cloud collapsed into the density and pressure needed to trigger nuclear fusion. Kirk never tired of its wonder.

And now here he was with McCoy, running a shuttlecraft directly into a sun. If anyone had told him that he would choose to do so, he would have laughed in disbelief.

Spock was alive inside that sun. He had to keep reminding himself of that as the sun grew ever larger on the screen. If all went as he hoped it would—as he had reason to believe that it should—the window would open at about a million kilometers, according to the data that had been recorded when the alien mobile had disappeared.

"We're coming up on the window," Kirk said.

McCoy nodded. "One moth leading another into the flame."

"Not the most consoling metaphor, Bones."

"Let's just hope it's not overly appropriate. I'll just keep telling myself that Spock went in this way, and so did the probe, and so will we."

The sun was swelling ever larger on the screen. Kirk's muscles tensed. He glanced down at one of the gauges on the console in front of him. The window would have to open any second now.

"Jim!" McCoy shouted. "We've gone past the window coordinates!"

"A little," Kirk replied, his voice catching in his throat. "Maybe it's not precisely situated. We'll go a bit farther."

But as the distance began to increase into thousands of kilometers sunward, he had the feeling that it was a hopeless effort. The window had opened once, to receive the mobile. Perhaps it would not open for another kind of object, a craft that the sun-core station's sensors—if it had sensors—would perceive as alien, and possibly hostile.

"Damn," McCoy said softly.

As Kirk turned the shuttlecraft away in a wide circle, he was imagining that Spock might remain to live out the rest of his life in the core of the Tyrtaean sun . . .

Spock looked up at the virtual sky and saw a deep purple shadow sweep across it. This shadow was even darker than the one he had seen earlier, and he sensed what it had to be. Someone from the *Enterprise* would be coming after him, trying to enter the sun-core station as he had, most likely in one of the starship's shuttlecraft.

Someone is coming for me, he said to the alien

gathering. You must let this vessel in. It will be the only way I shall be able to get out.

He waited a while for a response:

We must guard against the danger to ourselves. We are not yet ready to leave this station.

I assure you, Spock said, that there will be no danger to you.

We must consider further . . .

No one will harm you, Spock insisted. I promise you that. You can sense that what I tell you is true.

The aliens did not respond.

Those outside will be persistent, Spock continued. They will not leave me here without trying to ascertain exactly what has happened to me. Holding me will only provoke them into making more efforts to rescue me. You would be safer if you allowed me to depart.

There was a long pause. Spock quieted his thoughts, waiting for an answer.

We will risk it, came the long-delayed reply. There seem to be only two of your kind inside the incoming craft. We will allow it to enter.

I am grateful, Spock responded, then realized that they had said nothing about letting the shuttlecraft leave.

As Kirk ran the shuttlecraft at the sun for the second time, the brilliant sphere seemed to fall inward, almost as if something were trying to turn it inside out. A deep depression was forming at the sun's equator. The star swelled and took up the whole screen. But there was no heat, and all of the sensors and controls showed normal readings.

The depression began to look like a tunnel opening into the center of the star—

—and suddenly the shuttle was rushing through a fiery passage.

"It's opening for us," McCoy said. "This has to be the window—I wonder why it didn't open before."

Kirk watched the control panel and the screen warily, but the sensor readings remained normal before the awesome abnormality of the entrance into the star.

McCoy let out his breath, obviously stunned by the sight.

On and on the shuttlecraft plunged. The passage seemed endless, but a glance at the chronometer on his console told Kirk that only thirty seconds had elapsed. Suddenly it seemed to him that they were rushing straight down, and would emerge at any moment into a "basement" subspace underlaying the entire cosmos.

McCoy suddenly leaned forward. "Will you look at that!"

A blue space was opening up ahead. At first, its edges seemed amorphous, but then it snapped into sharp focus, as if he were gazing at a deep blue sky through a prismatic lens. Kirk glanced at the instrument panel again.

"Impossible," he said. "According to our instruments, we're no longer moving. We're disappearing from one point and then appearing in the next, with no distance being recorded, no velocity . . ."

"Spock would have a term for it," McCoy said.

"Quantum motion. I once heard it discussed in a lecture. Very different from warp motion."

McCoy cleared his throat. "You took the words right out of Spock's mouth."

The shuttlecraft was suddenly in the vast blue space. On the screen, just ahead, Kirk could see the rocky planetoid that was the alien mobile; the tiny cylinder that was the probe from the *Enterprise* hung near it in the shadowless blue space. The flat, indented metal surface of what looked like the previously discovered entrance to the mobile was clearly visible. The shuttlecraft began to slow and finally came to a stop against the mobile, as if settling into an invisible dock.

"We're up against the lock," Kirk said.

"It wouldn't open before, for Spock," McCoy reminded him. "It may not open now."

Kirk took out his communicator and flipped it open.

"Kirk to Spock."

There was no response.

He pressed the subspace communicator panel on the shuttle console.

"Kirk to Spock, do you read me?"

He heard nothing on either the shuttlecraft's communicator or his portable one.

"Maybe he's unable to use his communicator," McCoy said.

"The window opened for us," Kirk said. "Clearly something—some intelligence—is controlling it. That could be why we weren't allowed in at first. But we were permitted to enter this time."

"I hope it's not so we could be eliminated. Jim, we might already have learned more than the beings who built that mobile, or who created this space inside this sun, want us to know."

"We're still right against the lock," Kirk said, looking at his instrument panel. He glanced up at the screen again; to his surprise, the lock was now open. "Did you see it open, Bones?"

"No, I didn't. One second it was closed, and the next it was wide open."

"At least we won't have to cut our way in," Kirk said.

"Kinda makes me wonder." McCoy shook his head. "It's so damned convenient. They lure us in, and when we don't come back, maybe they lure the *Enterprise* itself in and get us all."

Kirk studied the physician's lined face. Leonard McCoy might be an emotional man, and inclined to expect the worst, but he wasn't given to delusions. There was a wary, fearful look in his eyes that Kirk had not seen before.

"Tell me exactly how you feel now, Bones," Kirk said.

"It's odd. I feel this overwhelming sense of danger now, but it seems to be coming from outside me. I feel fear and uneasiness, but not in my innards. So maybe it's up to you to use me

181

as . . . a sensor, a damned canary in the mine shaft!"

Spock might already be lost, Kirk thought. If some alien intelligence was trying to trap them, then the wisest course would be to leave immediately. If the shuttlecraft was not allowed to leave, he might still be able to send Sulu and the personnel on his ship a message not to follow him. No, Kirk decided; he would not leave before he knew what had happened to Spock.

"We have to go inside the mobile," Kirk said, "find Spock, and leave. There's nothing else we can do."

"I agree," McCoy said, "but if we get out of this, I'm never going to let that Vulcan forget the trouble his curiosity caused us."

"We'll wear protective suits," Kirk continued, "and take what precautions we can." He gazed at the screen, on which the vast blue space that surrounded the mobile glowed. "Hard to believe that we're inside a sun."

"It's a first," McCoy said.

Chapter Thirteen

KIRK CAME OUT as the shuttlecraft's lock opened, but halted in front of the mobile's open lock. The prospect of again entering the alien black and green interior suddenly repelled him; he recalled how disoriented he had been during his first trip inside. He closed his eyes for a moment.

"Jim," McCoy's voice said from the communicator inside Kirk's protective suit, "what is it?"

"Nothing." The eerie feeling faded. Kirk moved through the lock into the black corridor, with McCoy behind him.

"This open lock," McCoy said. "Still don't like it. Like an engraved invitation—feels as if they're just waiting for us."

"I expect they are," Kirk replied. "Maybe Spock has something to do with it." Maybe Spock was the bait. He pushed that thought aside, reached for his tricorder, and connected it to his suit's belt input.

He led the way through the jagged black corridor, pausing every few moments to check his tricorder readings. "He's here," he said, turning toward McCoy. "He's somewhere in this section of the mobile."

The physician's head bent forward as he peered at his own tricorder display inside his helmet. "Yes, but those life-sign readings look weaker than they should. Normal, but too weak."

Kirk moved forward; the readings were getting stronger. His first officer was somewhere ahead, but McCoy was right; Spock's life-sign readings still seemed low for a Vulcan, as if he were sedated or unconscious. "What do you make of those readings, Bones?"

"I don't like them. He's unconscious, possibly comatose."

"Hurry." Kirk picked up his pace, making one turn to his left, then another. Spock's tricorder life-sign readings grew fainter; he was going in the wrong direction. He retraced his steps, forcing himself to slow down, so as not to get lost. Occasionally he paused to close his eyes and shake off the feelings of disorientation.

"How do you feel?" he asked McCoy.

"Kinda dizzy—and I still have that odd feeling of dread coming from outside myself."

"Permission granted to return to the shuttlecraft," Kirk said, knowing that McCoy would stick with him.

"Not on your life."

Kirk made another turn, then stopped. Spock's protective suit—it had to be his suit—lay on the floor in front of him. He hurried toward it, swallowing his dismay, almost expecting to find the Vulcan still inside the suit.

He knelt and quickly examined the suit and helmet. Spock's backpack, with his portable subspace communicator, sat less than one meter away, against the wall.

"No damage," Kirk said. "Spock took it off and left it here."

"That, or someone forced him to take it off," McCoy murmured as Kirk stood up and continued forward.

The passageway grew more constricted. Kirk's tricorder readings indicated that he was getting closer to Spock, but the Vulcan's life-sign readings were still too low. The corridor would soon be too narrow for him to pass through. He went on until his broad, suited shoulders were caught between the walls, forcing him to stop.

"What now?" McCoy's voice said in his ear.

"Spock came through here. The tricorder readings tell me that he's up ahead."

"Then he took off his suit to get through that narrow space."

Kirk took a couple of steps backward, then turned to face McCoy. "We'll do the same."

McCoy was scanning with his tricorder. "The air's breathable."

"It was breathable when my team and I first came inside."

"But Spock was also thinner than you or me." Kirk heard the word *was* as a small explosion in his brain, and knew that Bones had instantly regretted saying it, but made no comment. "We might not be able to squeeze through that passage," McCoy said more softly.

Kirk removed his helmet, then began to take off his suit. McCoy had already removed his own helmet.

"You're always telling me that I could stand to lose a little weight," Kirk went on. "I should have listened to you."

"And I should have followed my own advice."

The two men removed their portable equipment, placed their suits near one wall, then turned toward the narrow passageway. Kirk hesitated, fearing suddenly that they might find Spock's body just beyond the constriction, collapsed like his empty suit.

He stepped forward without looking back at McCoy, almost afraid to see the doctor's expression—one of resignation, perhaps. At the narrowing he turned sideways, trying to squeeze through the tight, black passageway. The surface of the walls was as polished as obsidian, but almost seemed wet, pressing in on him as if it might suddenly become soft and give way.

"Can you make it, Jim?" McCoy asked.

"I'm trying." He managed to slip forward and was suddenly free. The corridor bent to the right. He turned to wait for McCoy.

The medical officer struggled through the narrow passage, then stumbled forward. Kirk reached out to steady him. "Easy, Bones."

"Thanks." McCoy squinted as he gazed down the corridor. "Is it my imagination, or does the light seem a little different up ahead?"

"It's not your imagination. It *is* a slightly different shade." Kirk stared at the strange glow up the corridor, noting the tinge of blue in the green.

They hurried forward and came to an open, oval entrance. Kirk peered inside and up toward what would be the ceiling; the chamber was shaped like a dome.

"Jim," McCoy said. Kirk lowered his eyes. "Do you see that?"

Near the center of the large chamber, in front of a panel shaped like a heptagon that rose from the black floor, stood a tall, shadowy figure, right arm raised, the palm of the right hand flat against the panel.

Kirk hurried across the floor. McCoy caught up with him as he reached Spock's side. Spock's pale skin had a more vivid green tinge to it, but that had to be the light; McCoy's face also had taken on a greenish hue. The Vulcan did not move; Kirk could not tell if he was breathing.

"Spock," Kirk said. "Spock?"

The Vulcan was motionless, as if frozen in place. Tiny bits of light flickered across the panel's surface.

McCoy quickly scanned Spock with his medical tricorder. "He's breathing," the medical officer said, "but respiration rate's much lower than normal."

"But what's wrong with him?"

"I'd almost think that he was in a trance or drugged state of some kind, except . . ." McCoy studied his tricorder. "His readings don't indicate any foreign substances or anything that looks like a drug. And his brain wave readings are similar to those of someone in deep concentration." He leaned closer to the inert Vulcan. Spock's eyes were open, unblinking, as expressionless as a blind man's. "He's alive, and apparently conscious, but he seems—almost paralyzed, but without the usual bodily distress of paralysis."

Kirk reached out and touched Spock's face, then his outstretched arm, but got no reaction. He gripped his friend's arm more tightly; the muscles were rigid. "Spock," he said softly, "can you hear me? What's happened to you?"

A menacing shadow, shaped like a stooping biped, covered most of the sky.

The shadow thundered, "Spock, can you hear me? What's happened to you?"

A friend, Spock told the aliens standing near him. This one, and the one who entered with him—they are my comrades. Spock hoped that his captors would believe him.

Captors?

Yes, Spock replied, for are you not holding me here?

Yes, we are, the aliens admitted, but only . . . until we are certain that you will do us no harm. Until we know that we are safe from you.

We will do you no harm, Spock insisted, gazing up at the shadow in the sky.

That we must determine for ourselves, the aliens whispered.

Spock's hand, Kirk noticed, was pressed carefully, almost precisely, against the panel. His elbow was slightly bent, his fingers spread; he had not put his hand against the surface in haste or from being startled, and there were no signs of force being used against him. He had put his palm against the alien wall deliberately.

"We've got to get him out of here," McCoy said.

"How?" Kirk touched Spock's arm again. "He's completely rigid. Even if we could move him, I don't think we could get him through that narrow passage." He clutched Spock's shoulders and pulled hard, but it was like trying to move a stone statue. Spock would have to have his right arm at his side to go through the narrows.

McCoy said, "He hasn't had a stroke, he's not in shock, there's no sign of brain injury or trauma, no sign of drugs, no sign of harm—but he doesn't seem to know we're here."

Kirk tried to think. "Bones, we don't know what's happened here."

"More like what *is* happening here," McCoy said.

"Exactly," Kirk said, feeling very inexact.

"He's being held by something," McCoy said, "and either he can't break free, or he doesn't want to."

Kirk suddenly realized that there was only one way to learn what it was that held Spock here. He had to do what Spock had obviously done to get himself into this state. He opened his right hand and stretched it toward the panel.

McCoy grabbed his wrist. "What are you doing, Jim? Are you insane?"

"Spock's alive. And we can't leave him here like this. I won't leave him."

McCoy released him and stepped back. "Of course we won't. I just hope that when we get him back, they haven't messed with his mind too much, that he'll be the same Spock." He paused. "Now there's a hell of a thing for me to admit." McCoy shook his head. "Don't take the chance, Jim. We'll get him out of here some other way."

"Sorry, Bones," Kirk said—and pressed his palm next to Spock's against the alien surface.

* * *

"Jim, no!" McCoy lunged toward his captain, but he was too late. Kirk's arm touched the panel and his body became rigid.

McCoy pulled at Kirk's arm, but was unable to move it. He grabbed Kirk by his broad shoulders and felt unyielding flesh.

Rigor mortis, he thought, and imagined the flesh rotting away from both of his friends, leaving only skeletons.

"Dammit, no," he muttered, stumbling back; his worst fears had proven correct. The aliens of the mobile had lured them inside to trap them. The peculiar feeling of dread nearly overcame him; he struggled to pull himself together.

He scanned Kirk with his tricorder, then did another scan of Spock. Low respiratory rate, slow and steady heartbeat, no sign of physical damage—indeed, all the symptoms of a deep, trancelike state. Kirk's eyes now held the same blind look as Spock's. McCoy peered into the two faces more closely. No, he concluded again, those eyes weren't completely blind and empty; there was a flickering of consciousness in them. He could almost imagine that Spock was deep in thought, and that Kirk was gazing at something wondrous just beyond the panel. They were together—somewhere.

He jostled Kirk's arm; there was no reaction. McCoy folded his arms and tried to guess at what was going on here. There seemed to be no overt threat, until one touched the panel. If the alien artifact did not affect the body, it clearly had an effect on the mind. There was a purpose behind all this, of that he was sure—but what?

McCoy reached for his communicator. Time to contact Sulu and Scott and tell them what had happened so far; maybe they would have some advice for him.

"McCoy to *Enterprise*." His communicator was silent, despite being patched into the subspace transmitter on his suit pack.

"McCoy to *Enterprise*."

Sulu might want to come in with another shuttle-craft and more personnel; he would warn the helmsman against that, tell him that the mobile had become a trap.

"Do you read me? McCoy to *Enterprise*."

The only sound from his communicator was like the hiss of a distant wind.

Spock had been able to contact the ship earlier, from inside this sun-core station, but now even the subspace link was cut off. Uhura had said that the channel was still wide open. When Spock had put his hand up against this panel, that must have been what had cut him off, why he had not responded to Uhura.

But this was different. Whatever controlled the mobile apparently did not want McCoy to communicate with the *Enterprise*, so now even the subspace link was blocked.

He tried to think of what to do now. Suddenly he had the urge to step up and place his own palm next to those of his two friends, to join them in their submission to whatever beckoned from beyond. . . .

But he resisted.

It seemed too much like death.

Kirk blinked—

—and saw Spock standing next to him.

"Welcome, Captain," Spock said. The Vulcan was clothed in his uniform, but his feet were bare and his top was a bit too short; he wore his belt, but his phaser and communicator were gone. Kirk looked down and saw that he was also in his uniform, but without his standard equipment. Under his bare feet, he saw red grass; the ground was warm against his soles.

He lifted his head and looked around at the alien landscape of red, grassy plains, a forest of black trees, orange cylinders surrounded by walls that crowned a hill above the strange forest, and a green river flowing down a red hillside. Then he saw the aliens standing nearby; there were six of them, all bipeds, hairless and with large eyes.

"The masters of this mobile," Spock said, "and we are visitors inside their culture." Kirk noted the respectful tones in Spock's voice.

"Why are we here?" Kirk asked.

"Our curiosity has made us intruders," Spock replied. "That's how they see us. You and I must try to convince them that we are not a threat to their way of life."

"Why would we ever wish to become a threat?" Kirk asked.

"They fear that we could become a threat despite our best intentions, Captain. They fear immigrants, so to speak, and I am sure that there are others in the Federation who would intrude out of curiosity."

Kirk nodded. "As we already have." The fear the aliens felt was not unjustified; other cultures had suffered damage and destruction at the hands of the well-intentioned. "Did you explain that we were trying to save them? Did you tell them that we thought their mobile might be a threat to the people of Tyrtaeus II?"

"Yes, I did, but I think that further explanation will be necessary."

Kirk had a feeling that it was going to take a lot more to free them than his promises of Federation respect.

He suddenly had the overpowering urge to put his right arm down, even though he could see that it was clearly at his side—here but not elsewhere.

Spock glanced at him. "I feel the same discomfort, Captain. I believe it comes from an imperfect match between our nervous systems and this virtual matrix. It was not made for us."

Kirk gazed at the alien delegation. They stared back at him, unmoving, and he could read no recognizable expression in their dark eyes. "What else can we do to reassure them that we mean them no harm."

"We *did* attack their mobile with our weapons."

"Only to protect the people of Tyrtaeus II. Only because we were afraid that the field around their mobile would affect this sun if they entered it. They must realize that."

"They do, Captain."

"If they can assure us without a doubt that their presence inside this sun will cause no harm to Tyrtaeus II, we will leave and trouble them no more."

"They have confirmed that their presence will not affect the star."

"Do you believe them?"

"It's difficult to say that I believe them. More to the point, I conclude that they have no motive to lie or do any harm."

"No motive that we understand," Kirk said.

Spock shook his head. "The logic of Occam's Razor, Captain. We must not proliferate assumptions beyond the facts before us. Events to this point indicate that the mobile failed to respond to us because it did not wish us to interfere with its purpose—namely to enter this sun-core station and dock here. It also failed to respond because it did not wish any of us to disturb the virtual world that the inhabitants have created for themselves. That seems more than adequate to explain all that has happened."

"So." Kirk faced the group of aliens and opened his arms. "Let's talk."

"What shall we say, Captain?" Spock asked. "To merely repeat our assurances will not be enough."

"Then what do you suggest?" Kirk asked.

"A good question, Captain."

McCoy cursed under his breath. He could not drag Kirk and Spock to the shuttlecraft without breaking off their arms, and he would not leave them here. He had a feeling that he would not be allowed to leave the mobile or the sun-core station anyway, even if he could have brought himself to abandon his comrades.

He grasped his communicator and flipped it open.

"McCoy to *Enterprise*," he murmured, not expecting to hear a voice from the ship, but not knowing what else to do. The sound like a distant wind answered him again; at last he slipped the communicator back onto his belt.

He would wait here, monitoring Kirk and Spock with his medical tricorder, hoping against hope that something unexpected would happen to free them. But then, suddenly, against all reason, he felt that joining the two in their trance was exactly what he should do. As that thought came to him, the strange feeling of dread faded a little.

He cursed again, slapped his palm hard against the panel, and held it there.

Between one blink of his eyes and the next, he was standing on a grassy red plain beside Kirk and Spock.

"Where in blazes are we?" McCoy asked, relieved to see his friends apparently alive and well, but startled and uneasy to find himself in the midst of a bizarre landscape, without his tricorder, barefooted and dressed in a badly fitted uniform. He turned his head slightly and saw six bipeds, humanoid but clearly not human.

As Spock updated him, McCoy surveyed the strange landscape. He was unnerved by the aliens who seemed so like—and yet so unlike—human beings, and by the rolling red plain of hills and forest of black trees that seemed somehow to want to be as much a part of him as outside.

"Now how the heck are we supposed to 'uncontact' these people?" McCoy said testily as Spock finished his explanation. "We won't be able to keep from reporting this. Once the existence of this mobile and this station are known, curiosity will eventually win out."

"Precisely," Spock said. "They're well aware that they cannot count on the promises of three lone individuals, or even the promises of everyone on board the *Enterprise*. They know that a massive culture stands behind us—one that is likely to be most curious about their technology."

You are different, a voice said.

McCoy heard the voice inside himself and knew that the aliens had spoken.

"Different?" McCoy asked, both speaking the words and thinking them.

You are also unlike this one, the one called

Spock. Your thoughts and his have a different quality. You are similar to the one called Captain Kirk, but we sense some differences between you two as well.

"Spock is a Vulcan," McCoy said, "who comes from another world than mine. He has human ancestry as well, but in upbringing and culture, he's Vulcan."

Spock turned toward him and lifted a brow slightly.

"Captain Kirk and I," McCoy went on, "are human beings from a planet called Earth. We share a culture, with minor variations, but I suppose you could say that we have different personalities. Anyway, humans of the same species often disagree, if that helps you any."

Yet all of you are what you call friends, the aliens murmured.

McCoy turned toward his companions. "Yes," he admitted, "we are all friends. It's why I entered this virtual reality of yours—to find my friends. It wasn't because of curiosity about you, or an attempt to learn any of your secrets—it was to find my friends and bring them back safely to our ship."

"And I came here to find Spock," Kirk said.

We sense that the motives of Spock are other than yours, the aliens whispered, that his curiosity brought him to us.

"That is true," Spock said, "and I know how much you fear the curiosity of others."

The alien bipeds did not respond.

"But I have satisfied some of my curiosity," Spock added.

The aliens remained silent. Spock glanced at Kirk, then toward McCoy, and McCoy guessed from the look in the Vulcan's eyes that he had come to some sort of decision.

"I spoke to you earlier about a planet called Talos IV," Spock said, "the world whose inhabitants create imaginary realms with their thoughts. The Federation has forbidden any Starfleet vessel to go there. Any Federation citizen who journeys to Talos IV risks the death penalty, a punishment almost never imposed for other offenses. It is my belief that the Federation can be convinced to take similar steps to protect you. Indeed, I am willing to plead your case if you will allow me and my comrades to leave."

Your reasoning is flawed, the alien delegation responded. The restrictions of your Federation did not prevent you from returning to that forbidden world of Talos IV on an errand of mercy. And we are not like those you call Talosians. Their illusions were a trap. Ours are not.

"I shall offer another argument, then," Spock said, "one that should convince you that letting us go is your only rational choice. We are officers on one of the most important of our Starfleet vessels. The Federation and Starfleet went to some trouble and expense to train us, and we have, if I may say so, won a few honors and some renown for our service. If you let us go, we can be your advocates and plead your case. If you keep us here, you will only guarantee that others will continue to come after us, and will not leave you alone until they find out what happened to us."

The aliens were silent. Moments passed, growing longer until McCoy began to worry that the delegation might never communicate with them again.

Kirk said at last, "I don't think they liked your words about pleading their case. Sounds like it's still to be decided."

"Yes, Captain—but it is also the case that, if they do not let us go, they increase the likelihood of what they seem to fear most, namely intrusion and contact with outsiders."

"Well, I now have a strong feeling," Kirk said, "that they've already found out all that they need to know about us to ensure their privacy. Their problem will be settled by means other than talk."

The aliens continued to stare past the three, as if completely uninterested in anything they now had to say.

"That is an interesting leap, Captain," Spock said. "And what exactly do you mean?"

"I think Jim means that they have our number," McCoy replied.

Spock lifted both brows. "Number?"

"That they've figured out what we're capable of doing, what kinds of motivations we have, and what they have to do in order to protect themselves from us."

You may go.

McCoy was startled. He glanced at Kirk and Spock, and saw that they had also heard the words.

You may go, the aliens repeated, and McCoy felt a great tiredness and heaviness in his right arm. As he relaxed it, the world dissolved around him, the red grass and black trees became ghostly, and he thought he saw the aliens move away from him in discontinuous motions, disappearing and then reappearing before they faded completely from view, and he was suddenly standing again in front of the alien panel.

Needles of pain pricked his right arm; he swung it back and forth as he flexed his fingers. Next to him, Kirk was massaging his own arm, but Spock's hand was still against the panel. He was as motionless as he had been when they first found him.

McCoy stepped toward Spock and clutched at his right arm; his muscles were still rigid. "Jim, he's still there. He won't let go."

Kirk took the Vulcan by the shoulders. "Spock, come out!"

McCoy grabbed Spock's right wrist tightly with one hand while holding his shoulder with the other. Kirk was pulling at Spock's left shoulder and arm. The Vulcan's body was stiff and unyielding, but they managed to drag him back from the panel on his feet. The Vulcan muscles under McCoy's hand loosened, and the figure became unsteady. Then Spock shook himself and found his footing, flexed his right arm, and his familiar contemplative but distant expression returned to his face.

"Doctor McCoy," Spock said, "there was no danger and no need to move me. I would have been with you and the captain in a few moments."

"Spock," McCoy growled, "this is no time to stop and smell the roses. Or the virtual vegetation. Or whatever the heck they call . . ."

"Doctor, I was merely attempting to ascertain . . ."

Kirk rolled his eyes. "Gentlemen, you are welcome to continue this discussion—aboard the *Enterprise*. For now, however, I suggest that we get the hell out of here while we can."

Chapter Fourteen

THEIR SUITS AND BACKPACKS were where they had left them, just beyond the extreme narrowing of the corridor. Kirk was suddenly apprehensive, imagining that the walls might close in and prevent exiting.

He pushed through the tight passage, then found his suit.

Spock squeezed through the passage after him, then reached back to pull McCoy through. "We'll put those suits back on," Kirk said. "I don't want to take any more chances than necessary."

McCoy picked up one of the suits. "'You may go,' they told us. Maybe they just wanted us out of their virtual reality, but have decided they're going to keep us inside this thing."

"Doctor," Spock said, "we have no reason to

assume that, or even that the inhabitants of the mobile ever meant to harm us. Given that we were the intruders, it can be argued that they have shown some forbearance."

Here we go again, Kirk thought. *Nice to know things are getting back to normal.* "Mr. Spock," he interrupted, a bit more forcefully than he had intended. "I'm assuming that Vulcan senses are more trustworthy in this terrain. You lead the way."

Spock went ahead, occasionally reaching out to press a gloved hand against the walls. Kirk followed, with McCoy just behind him. If the aliens were planning to move against them, or to imprison them here, they would soon know. His hand reflexively moved toward the phaser at his waist, and then he remembered that his weapon was useless here.

Spock paused to scan the area ahead. "The aliens are not attempting to mislead us," he said. "The tricorder readings are quite clear and steady."

The Vulcan moved on. One bend in the corridor, then another; Kirk would have found his way back without Spock, but it would have taken him longer, even with the tricorder readings. The uneasiness and dizziness that had troubled him on his first trip inside the mobile was gone, but he still felt disoriented by the twisting, irregular passageways.

Spock slowed his pace slightly, then reached for his tricorder again. "We are going in the right direction, Captain," he said as he scanned. "The shuttlecraft is not far away."

The aliens had created a virtual world indistinguishable from reality; they were certainly capable of sending spurious, genuine-seeming signals to a tricorder. Kirk shook off the thought, keeping his gaze on Spock's booted feet as he followed the Vulcan along the passageway.

"The exit is open," Spock announced.

Startled, Kirk looked up and saw that they had come to the lock.

Spock led the way through the open lock and into the shuttlecraft. Kirk took his position at the controls and saw that the instrument readings were unchanged.

"Everything's fine," Kirk said as Spock sat down at his right. "Our lock is closed. Almost makes you wonder."

"Yeah," McCoy said from behind him. "We're back in that chamber, still pressing our palms against that panel. Maybe our air lock is open, and we don't know it. Simple way to kill us as we leave."

"It is unlikely that this is all an illusion," Spock said. "It would be pointless to give us all this if they wished to harm us."

McCoy sighed. "Unless they're toying with us, or have a very strange sense of humor."

"That would not be humor, Doctor—it would be malice, and malice rarely manifests itself as an unalloyed motive, even in human beings. All that I can see here, until proven wrong, is that we have simply been allowed to leave—encouraged to leave, in fact. Suspicions require some evidence in order to be taken seriously."

"Bones, Spock—get ready for our departure," Kirk said. He waited, trying to convince himself that Spock had to be right. They had no evidence that the aliens meant to harm their visitors, even though they had the means to do so. The mobile was clearly capable of more decisive, even over-whelming action against the *Enterprise*. He considered how much the inhabitants of the mobile now knew about the starship's capacities, and con-cluded that they were aware that his ship was not the equal of their mobile. Given what they might have done, the aliens had responded minimally to the *Enterprise*'s actions.

"You have a point, Spock," McCoy said, sound-ing as though he hated to admit it. "They probably could have finished us off as soon as we fired our first phaser at them."

Kirk set the course control program to reverse the shuttlecraft's entrance into the sun-core, and waited as he gazed at the viewscreen to see whether they would be allowed to leave after all.

Then the alien mobile suddenly fell away on the screen, shrinking rapidly, and in a few moments hung in the deep blue field of the otherspace interior. Kirk pictured the reality of the star's inferno, heat born of gravitational pressure, wait-ing to break into this haven.

As the shuttlecraft obeyed its return program, the deep blue began to fade on the viewscreen. Kirk glanced at the controls and noted that the velocity reading had again stopped on the control display. Quantum motion returned as the shuttlecraft blinked from point to point, appearing and disappearing across the distance to the invisible exit.

"Fascinating," Spock murmured. "We are being projected outward by a very sophisticated tractor beam, whose origin must be in the mobile."

"In the same way as we were brought in," Kirk added.

A starry space was opening up ahead. Its edges were amorphous, but suddenly the circular patch came into sharp focus, and grew to cover the whole screen. Standard velocity readings appeared on the control panel as the shuttlecraft shot out of the sun.

"Apparently quite routine—for our hosts," Spock said.

Behind Kirk, McCoy let out a sigh. "Amazing," he said, "so amazing that I wonder if we can keep the promise Spock made to the aliens. Starfleet's going to want to find out how this technology works."

Spock glanced back at the physician. "Somehow, Doctor, I do not think the aliens would be allowing us to leave if they had only our word with which to protect themselves."

Kirk felt apprehension stir inside him again. "Shuttlecraft to *Enterprise*," he said. "Kirk here."

"*Enterprise* here," Sulu's voice replied. "Captain, we just sighted you coming directly out of the sun."

Kirk said, "We're coming in. Spock's alive and well, and Dr. McCoy is with us. I've got one hell of a report to make, Mister Sulu."

"Spock is safe!" Uhura's voice cried out. "Captain, there are a lot of smiling faces on this bridge."

Kirk grinned, happy to hear his ship's welcome, but he was unable to believe that it was all over. If anything, the people of the mobile had to be more uncertain than before. It remained for them to deal with that uncertainty.

How they would do that was still to come. *He* was certain of that.

Chapter Fifteen

"SOMETHING'S INSIDE OUR SUN," Myra Coles said, "and not just that mobile, but an entire alien facility apparently designed to service it, with a technology far more sophisticated than ours. Yet you say that we're in no danger."

"None that we can discern." Kirk rested his hands on the table. "They assured us of this."

Her eyes widened in disbelief. "Can we believe them?"

The Tyrtaean leader had seemed almost as eager as his crew to welcome Kirk and his two fellow officers back to the *Enterprise*. He had given everyone on the bridge a brief summary of what they had discovered inside the sun, and described their encounter with the aliens. Myra had not objected when he ordered everyone who had been on duty to get some rest; she had even smiled at him before leaving the bridge with her aide.

Then she had requested a meeting with him after he had been awake less than an hour, before he could even begin entering a full report of the incident in his captain's log. She had been waiting for him here in the briefing room with Wellesley Warren, when he and Spock arrived.

Well, he told himself, he should have known that her momentary warmth and friendliness wouldn't last. Her obligations to her people were pressing in on her again.

Spock said, "We accepted the assurances we were given, Miss Coles, but we did not do so blindly. A deep scan of your sun reveals no evidence of any danger. In fact, after comparing this scan with our other records of this sun's activity, even solar flares seem to have declined in frequency and duration. In fact, your sun seems more stable than ever."

"But what about the long term?" Myra Coles looked from Spock to Yeoman Rand, who was sitting at Kirk's left, then focused her gray eyes on Kirk.

"There may be problems with any star over the long run," Kirk said.

"Based on what we have seen," Spock added, "it would be a mistake to ascribe any future increase in solar activity to the presence of the alien mobile. Since the station may have been there for some time without altering your sun's activity, we can infer that it is not likely to do so in the foreseeable future. In fact, it may have been beneficial, and may continue to be so."

The woman let out her breath. "So what now, James—Captain? Are we to share our system with this alien artifact, embedded in our sun?"

Kirk glanced at Spock.

"The question is academic," the Vulcan said, "since we are unlikely to be able to do anything about it. Our fears about the alien mobile appear to have been groundless."

Myra Coles shook her head. "They may not be hostile now. What's to stop them from turning on us especially if they feel threatened again? I don't know if this is going to draw our malcontents closer to the Federation, or drive them even further from it. On the one hand, we could argue that if there is a possible threat, we may need Starfleet and the Federation to defend us later. On the other hand, this may bring even more people to join with the anti-Federationists in demanding an independent colony in another system, since they will surely believe we'd be safer somewhere else. We certainly won't have any political stability on Tyrtaeus II for a while. Aristocles made that very clear in his latest subspace message." She looked down for a moment. "And all I can do is keep insisting that there's little reason for the aliens to be hostile, and every reason to assume that all they want is to be left to themselves. Maybe that message will get through if I insist on it long enough and the aliens don't do anything to cast doubt on it. They're not so different from us that way, wanting to be left alone."

Spock nodded. "Indeed. That is an observation that should carry some force with your people."

"Still, we can't be certain that there will never be any danger to our world."

Spock leaned forward and rested his elbows on the table top. "Certainty is not to be had about anything, Miss Coles. But I am as certain as is possible under these circumstances. What happened may be easily summarized." He paused.

"Please continue, Mr. Spock," Wellesley Warren said. "For the record."

"By attempting to explore the mobile, we stimulated its defensive programs, which are run by a very advanced artificial intelligence that has given up on changing the given universe. Instead, it has achieved the experience of omnipotence, by linking the output of its minds to the AI input. This culture does not crave the secrets of a transcendent universe, which can never be unraveled because one cannot reach the end of a standing infinity—that is what they believe our universe to be. But do not misunderstand—they know enough about the physical universe to attain what they wish."

"Mr. Spock—" Myra Coles began.

Spock glanced briefly in her direction, but continued: "A culture that has withdrawn into virtual worlds must, by its very nature, be shy and secretive, and protective of its security. It was apparently time for this one to renew its energy resources when we came along, so it began its journey toward the Tyrtaean sun, which alerted us that it was not a natural object. It became clear to them when we tried to contact them that they might become an object of study, so their defensive systems went into action."

"Then we can't make any overtures of friendship to them?" Wellesley Warren asked.

"I think not," Spock replied. "They would be rejected. There will be no exchange of embassies."

Myra Coles fidgeted, tapping her fingers against the table top; her face betrayed her agitation.

"Then from what you say," Wellesley Warren went on, "we must tolerate them here, in our home system, and never learn anything more about them. Live and let live. Well, we Tyrtaeans, of all people, have to respect that."

Spock nodded. "To repeat, nothing can be done about it."

The Tyrtaean man sighed. "And we can't protest to them, obviously."

"Perhaps they also originated in this system," Spock said. Kirk thought that extremely doubtful, but kept his doubts to himself. "If so, they have as much right to live in it as you do—perhaps more of a right. It seems clear, however, that they are willing to share it with you."

"As long as they keep to themselves," Myra Coles murmured, "and allow us to do the same, we can hardly object to that. But I'd feel a lot better if we could know for sure that they would never become a threat."

"Miss Coles," Spock said, "I have more reasons than I have given thus far for assuming that the aliens of the mobile are no threat to any of us now." He cast a sidelong glance at Kirk. There was something in the Vulcan's eyes that Kirk had not seen before. Anger? Concern? Chagrin? But Spock would not have such feelings; he certainly would never acknowledge them.

"These reasons are as follows," Spock continued. "Had the aliens spoken only to me, they might still have felt threatened, and might still have considered taking some sort of strong action against us—not because they suspected any violent intent on my part, but because they had learned that my curiosity had motivated me to take a great risk. They had seen earlier that a team from the *Enterprise* entered their habitat for the sole purpose of exploring the unknown. To protect themselves, they might then have decided to destroy anyone else who could have led others to them. They might have believed that our curiosity outweighed everything else, and therefore that it posed a great danger to their safety. But they did nothing."

Kirk sat back in his chair. He had known from the beginning that there were risks in exploring the mobile; he had not wanted to dwell on how high the stakes might be.

"I believe," Spock went on, "that it was the arrival of Captain Kirk and Doctor McCoy that caused the aliens to revise their judgment of us. The captain and the doctor came there, not out of curiosity, or because they were following orders, but to find their friend. The aliens learned that, for us, other things could outweigh curiosity, and in a much more effective way than if I had simply insisted on that fact. I think that may be one reason they decided to let us go."

Kirk was struck by Spock's words. It probably irritated him, Kirk thought, to admit openly that both logic and human feeling, and not reason alone, might have been required to free him from the mobile.

"Still," Wellesley Warren said, "there's a lot to be curious about, and much the aliens could show us. Yes, we do have to leave them be, but there's so much we could learn from them."

"Perhaps they can teach us something anyway," Myra Coles said, a pensive look on her face. "Here is a race that has turned so far inward that they haven't just cut themselves off from other intelligences, they've also retreated from the universe around them. Their kind of isolation is a prison, in a way. All that power, and what have they used it for? To shut themselves up, to be even more fearful of the outside whenever it intrudes on them. Maybe we should see their example as a warning."

"I wouldn't mind asking them some questions," Wellesley Warren said, "before they retreat into their isolation completely."

"Nor would I," Spock said, "but at the moment, we have no direct communications with the mobile."

"And we must abide by the promise we made to them," Kirk added, "to recommend to Starfleet and the Federation Council that all contact with these aliens be prohibited, at least for now, while leaving us open to contact with them later, if *they* choose."

"Of course, but I fear that may not work," Myra Coles said. "Curiosity drew you. It will attract others. I don't know if the Federation Council will agree to such a ban. Even if they do, some individuals will try to violate it, if the word gets out. I wonder how that will affect my people. Tyrtaeus II would be a natural base for anyone who wants to investigate the mobile. And I doubt that only Federation members will be interested. The Romulans might decide that the potential of this alien technology is worth violating a treaty and crossing the Neutral Zone to this system."

That thought had already crossed Kirk's mind. "We're pledged to defend Tyrtaeus II," he said. "This doesn't change that—it just gives us another reason to honor that promise."

She gazed directly at him. "In any case, I will now have to go back and tell Aristocles and my people that we must live with this predicament. Some, perhaps most, will believe that we provoked this situation and that the aliens may show future hostilities toward us as a result. Others will, with some justification, fear a Romulan incursion into our space. They will look for someone to blame."

"But—" Kirk searched for something to say as he realized that this might be the end of everything for Myra—her position, her career, perhaps her life. Janice Rand gazed at the Tyrtaean woman, sympathy in her eyes. "I'll do everything I can to help you," Kirk said, hearing how useless that sounded. "When your people see my full report, they'll know that, if anything, you were trying to be extremely cautious. We can appeal—"

"Bridge to Captain Kirk," Sulu's voice said over the intercom.

Kirk leaned toward the small screen in front of him. "Kirk here."

Sulu said, "We're reading some activity in the sun, sir."

Kirk got to his feet. "I'll be right there." His stomach clenched as he imagined that Myra Coles's fears might be realized, and that the mobile's presence had indeed affected the star. He glanced across the table as he started toward the door, with Spock just ahead of him. Myra Coles stared after him with her lips pressed tightly together; her expression seemed a mixture of bitter satisfaction at having been right after all and uncertainty and fear about what might happen now.

Spock was out of the lift and hastening toward his station, where Ali Massoud and Cathe Tekakwitha awaited him, as Kirk hurried to his station. McCoy stood near it, his face flushed; he had obviously hurried to the bridge from sick bay.

"Any change?" Kirk asked as he sat down behind Sulu and Riley.

"None, Captain," Riley replied.

"Something's moving inside the sun," Massoud said. "That much we know. Deep scanning of the sun now."

The turbolift door whispered open again. Janice Rand came toward Kirk's station, followed by Myra Coles and her aide.

"I believe I know what may be happening," Spock said.

Kirk turned in his chair to see Spock peering at his instruments. "What?"

Spock looked up for a moment. "The alien mobile is about to emerge from the sun."

"Put it up on the viewscreen," Kirk ordered, facing forward.

The sun's glare suddenly filled the bridge with filtered light. The screen pulled in on a tiny black dot on the sun's equator. The dot swelled as it fled from the star.

"It's accelerating," Spock said. "Deep scan of

the sun reveals that the sun-core station is collapsing at this very moment."

Myra Coles clasped her hands together.

"It's gone, Captain," Spock said, "and with scarcely a ripple showing anywhere in the sun."

"Almost as if it were never there at all," McCoy murmured at Kirk's side.

"Incredible," Myra Coles said, sounding both disappointed and relieved at the same time. "I wouldn't have believed it if I hadn't seen it myself."

"Indeed," Spock responded. "I now conclude that the sun-core station was merely a temporary structure, opened solely for the replenishing of the mobile's energy."

"Amazing," Wellesley Warren said. "What power they must have!"

Kirk thought of what Spock had said in the briefing room, and knew what he would have to do now to prove to the aliens that they were safe from interference; there were many ways to show one's friendship and good will. He glanced toward the Vulcan for a moment. Spock was looking back at him with an expression that said: I know what you will do, Captain, and I know why.

McCoy saw the conspiratorial look on Jim Kirk's face as he looked toward Spock, and wondered what the captain would do now. "Mr. Sulu," Kirk said, turning around and leaning forward in his command chair, "make speed to pursue."

"Aye, aye, Captain."

"I agree," Spock said from his station. "We must follow them as far as we can."

Insanity, McCoy thought, and that Vulcan was going along with it. He glanced at the Coles woman, who was clearly sharing his doubts; her eyes were wide with bewilderment.

McCoy moved closer to the captain. "Jim," he said in a low voice, "are you sure you know what you're doing?"

Kirk looked up at him. "Yes, Bones, I do. Right now, it seems like a good idea to follow the mobile and see where it's heading."

"And to finally provoke it into a hostile response? Shouldn't we leave well enough alone?"

"We have no evidence that the aliens will engage in any hostile action." Kirk turned toward the viewscreen. "In fact, we never had any such evidence."

"But Spock admitted—" Myra Coles began, then paused. "He said that your actions were responsible for awakening its defensive systems."

"Which have been quite benign," Kirk said, "and have treated our attempts at contact with some consideration. They could have acted against us with devastating force—they clearly have the technology to do so. They haven't. They don't have to."

"They haven't yet," the Tyrtaean woman said softly. McCoy waited for her to say more, but she was silent. She would be thinking that Jim Kirk was again playing with the lives of an entire solar system. McCoy could only hope that she was wrong—that they were both mistaken.

"Captain," Myra Coles said, "are you actually going to try to catch them?"

Kirk was about to answer when Spock said, "We shall keep pace at a discreet distance."

Kirk heard Spock's statement with some surprise. His words were directed at the Tyrtaeans and smacked of diplomacy on the Vulcan's part; or was it simply his usual rational caution? Spock would want to follow the mobile out of his natural curiosity, but his logical mind would also urge him to be prudent.

"Still accelerating," Sulu said.

"Keep up with it," Kirk replied.

"They're going to warp one," Riley said.

"Keep up," Kirk said.

"Warp one point one!" Sulu called out, clearly unable to contain the excitement in his voice. "It's going to go to warp two, Captain."

Kirk suddenly had an inkling of what was going to happen. "Pursue, Mister Sulu."

"Aye, aye, Captain. Now at warp two."

"James," Myra Coles asked, "why are we in pursuit?"

He glanced up at the Tyrtaean leader and said, "It's not really pursuit, since we don't aim to catch them."

"Then what is it?" Myra demanded.

Kirk shrugged. "We're . . . observing."

"Warp three," Sulu said.

On the screen, the alien was fleeing with an ever-increasing velocity, yet it seemed stately and relaxed to Kirk, as if hardly straining.

"Jim, what are you doing?" McCoy muttered.

"Spock," Kirk said, "are you still thinking what I am?"

"Yes, Captain."

"Warp four," Sulu announced.

Kirk gazed at the viewscreen, thinking about the alien culture cradled in the mobile. As an old poem said—but he couldn't quite remember the words—these people had remade their world nearer to their heart's desire. But had they truly done so? From what he had seen, the outward safety of their culture was secured, was being even further secured as the mobile fled. But what had they lost, in turning away from an intractable universe? Was the real universe to be preferred to a great, creative, inward life? Spock would have some views about that.

"Warp five!" Sulu shouted.

"And they're still way out in front of us," Riley said.

Kirk thought of the alien panel in the domed oval chamber against which he had pressed his palm. It had to be a durable matrix of some kind, to contain a virtual plenum woven of mind designs. Outwardly, the panel wall seemed to be nothing much at all, but in the flow of electrons, deep down among the quanta, minds reveled with power over their desires . . .

"Warp six, Captain," Sulu said.

"Continue, Mister Sulu." Kirk sat back, watching the universe rush by the *Enterprise*. How did that poem go?

"Seven!" Sulu said.

"Eight!"

"Continue in pursuit."

"Nine!" Sulu shouted.

"Engineering to bridge!" Scotty's voice called out over the communicator.

"Kirk here."

"What in blazes is going on up there, Captain? We'll start to break up at just past ten!"

"I know what I'm doing, Scotty."

"I hope so," the engineer muttered.

"Ten, Captain!" Sulu's voice rose. "They're at warp ten!"

"Take it to ten and hold, Mister Sulu."

"Holding steady, sir."

For a long time, there was silence on the bridge. Kirk watched the mobile on the screen. The alien was holding at warp ten, almost as if it was reluctant to insult the *Enterprise*. The poem that he was trying to recall refused to come back to him.

Then the mobile began to shrink against the blackness of space and stars.

"It's going to eleven," Sulu said in a cracking voice. "Twelve. Thirteen. Fourteen. Fifteen—Captain, it's way off our scale!"

And then it was gone—leaving only the usual warp of space rushing by the ship. Warp ten suddenly seemed slow to Kirk.

As he gazed with awe and admiration at the empty screen, he imagined the alien mobile riding a wave of immense nonEinsteinian velocity, doing what his beloved *Enterprise* could not do and would never be able to do—go anywhere in the universe, touch any star. Yet those who traveled inside it had turned inward, into themselves, and all the vast outwardness of the cosmos was to them only a cloak for their dream-life.

"Plot its course," Kirk called out.

"Somewhere toward the center of the galaxy," Riley replied. "Course untraceable."

"Reduce speed," Kirk said as he sat back. "Return course to Tyrtaeus II."

"Captain," Scotty said from engineering, "it was a marvel! I wouldn't even call what they have warp engines. They were literally rolling up the universe before them like a carpet!"

"Advanced warp engines," Kirk said. "We'll have them one day."

"Don't try to console me, Captain," Scotty said. "I know my betters when I see them, and they were a glory to behold!"

"Yes," Kirk said. "It's what you can do with the power of a sun to send you on your way."

Myra Coles was looking at him wonderingly. "And what, may I ask, did that chase prove?" she asked.

Kirk glanced aft. "Mr. Spock?" he said. "Perhaps you should answer Miss Coles's question."

Spock left his post and came to stand at Kirk's right. Sulu and Riley turned at their forward stations to look at the Vulcan; Uhura turned around at her station. McCoy frowned at Kirk's left, as if ready to take issue with anything Spock said.

"Gladly, Captain," Spock said. "The captain suspected, as did I, that the people of the alien mobile wished to make sure of their privacy and safety, and there was only one way for them to do that—by leaving this system in a manner that would preclude our following them. They would have been extremely trusting, even foolish, to rely only on our pledge that they would be left to continue their lives in peace. And the Federation would have had the added burden of forbidding all contact with the mobile and enforcing that injunction, as it did with Talos IV—although I think the two cases are somewhat different. . . ."

"But why did the captain pursue them?" Wellesley Warren asked impatiently.

"I'll answer that myself," Kirk said. "There were two aims to be accomplished. The first was to see what the mobile could do, to *know* firsthand what kind of science and technology we were facing. Second, to show the alien mobile that we could not catch them, that they could protect themselves from us by escaping from us completely. Otherwise, they might reasonably have had doubts about their security."

"You thought of all of that?" the Tyrtaean leader asked, with a hint of newfound respect in her voice. "But what if you *had* been able to catch them? Were you so sure that you couldn't?"

Kirk nodded. "I suspected that we couldn't catch them, but I wasn't completely certain. Would you have preferred for us to leave a doubt in their minds, to have them always wondering whether we could go out and find them? I was prepared to slow down and show an 'inability' to catch them, if it had become necessary."

Myra Coles sighed and nodded. "You're right. With that level of science and technology, they could have done whatever they wished with us, if they felt sufficiently threatened. I must admit it—what you've done has probably ensured the safety of my people. The aliens have learned that we are willing to let them be, but also that we lack the capacity to go after them. They are safe, too."

Kirk could not help smiling. "You took the words right out of my mouth."

She tilted her head. "So in effect, their parting message to us is, we have our lives and you have yours. Good-bye."

"I couldn't have said it better," Kirk said, meeting her open gaze and realizing that she was telling him the same thing on behalf of herself and her own world.

"Well, I say good riddance," McCoy said.

Kirk paid no attention to the comment. He wanted to tell Myra that Federation colonies had to be competitive, suspicious, even for a time inward-looking and isolationist, in order to grow, to develop the cultural and biological individualities that human and humanoid life spreading across the star systems of the galaxy might one day need to keep their cultures vital. In that sense, the Tyrtaean antiFederationists were right, but they did not need a complete break to achieve their ends; the Federation was willing to leave its member worlds alone. Myra might call his words Federation paternalism, and mock him for his show of generosity, even though she clearly believed the same thing herself. He would say that in the short term it might seem like paternalism, but in the long term it meant survival and growth . . . and she would say that words were cheap . . . and he would tell her fervently that he believed every word of the Federation's ideals . . . and she would look into his eyes and know it was right and true. . . .

But instead of the exchange of words and feelings that might have been in the duet he wished for, Kirk said, "I understand. The future of the Federation depends on its colonies and member worlds, Miss Coles."

Myra Coles smiled at his formality. "Yes, Captain, of course."

Chapter Sixteen

ARISTOCLES WAS IN the main square to meet Wellesley and Myra when they beamed down from the
Enterprise. Myra had insisted that they arrive by
themselves. That was practical, Wellesley supposed, given that James Kirk's crew had better
things to do than accompany them to Callinus, but
perhaps Myra had not wanted to provoke Aristocles Marcelli any more than necessary. Tact
suggested that she not come home with a group of
Starfleet officers.

Aristocles stepped forward to greet them. "Welcome back, Myra and Wellesley," he said in a calm
voice. One corner of his mouth twitched, and his
dark eyes were rimmed with red; he did not look as
though he had been sleeping well.

"Greetings, Aristocles," Myra said, "I'm impatient to get back to work, but there is one matter we have to discuss first. The people aboard the *Enterprise* could use some rest and relaxation. I thought we might invite them to spend some time here."

"For relaxation?" Aristocles said, as if uncertain of the word's meaning.

Myra's face was composed. "They will perform their duties more efficiently later if they take some time off now."

"Time off." Aristocles looked disdainful. "Too much relaxation only makes people soft."

"That depends on one's choice of recreation," Myra said. "A hike in the hills, a mountain climb, a long swim in one of our lakes—I fail to see how such activities weaken a person."

"We had more than enough contact with Starfleet while Kirk's people were restoring our data base," Aristocles said as he led them toward the Callinus Administrative Center. "I fail to see why—"

"Afraid they'll contaminate us?" Myra asked. For a moment, Wellesley thought she might smile. "I think our developing culture is strong enough to withstand a bit more contact with others. Sometimes too much isolation can produce an unfounded distrust—in the absence of any contact, it's easy to imagine all kinds of things about people one doesn't know. I've been distrustful of Federation officials and Starfleet officers myself, but—"

"Proud of yourself, aren't you?" Aristocles stopped and turned to face them; Wellesley halted next to Myra, shocked by the venom in Aristocles's voice. "You'll do the Federation's work for them. You've done their work for them all along. You're nothing better than a Federation agent yourself."

Wellesley glanced around the square. It was only an hour after dawn, and most of the people in Callinus would already be at work or at school, but a few people were watching them from across the way.

"You know better than that, Aristocles." Myra's voice was low, but strong. "There's no shame in being grateful to someone who has rendered us a service, and James Kirk and his people have done that. If they hadn't been here to help with our data base, we would never have known what the mobile was, and that it wasn't a threat to us." She lifted a brow. "Not that you couldn't have used doubts about it to further your own ends. You could have argued that, since an alien presence in this system might be a menace, we should abandon this world and start a new colony somewhere else, independent of the Federation. Perhaps you would even have insisted that our safety required that we cut ourselves off from all contact with the outside."

Aristocles's face flushed with anger; Wellesley saw him struggling to control himself. "I'll still appeal to the Federation for a colony, and for independence," he said. "Many will support such a plea."

So it was out in the open at last, Wellesley thought with relief. To stand or fall.

"Perhaps not as many as once would have supported it," Myra said softly, "and I don't know if permission will be easily granted for a small colony that can't be viable. And you don't have the means to start it without Federation support."

At the top of the Administrative Center's wide stone stairway, Myra's other three aides were waiting in front of one open doorway. Aristocles's four aides stood with them. Myra would want them all at the meeting when they discussed what to do about shore leave for the *Enterprise's* crew. What was decided there, Wellesley knew, would be the first test of which leader, Myra or Aristocles, now had the upper hand, and whether the Tyrtaeans would have a chance to work out their differences. Ironically, the test would come over what was in reality a small matter.

"Don't I have support?" Aristocles said. "I needn't go to the Federation for support—I can find enough by myself." He let out his breath. "You think things will go your way now. Even my aides think more highly of you after listening to your most recent report. One of them even dared to say that we might benefit from more contact with Starfleet and other Federation worlds."

"You should listen to your aides," Myra said. "Our encounter with the mobile seems to demonstrate that quite clearly. You were the one who recommended that Tyrtaeans be aboard the *Enterprise* when the mobile was explored, so even you have conceded that we and the Federation sometimes have to work together. Surely you were thinking of our world's interests and not just of your own when you made that suggestion to me? Perhaps you deserve a little of the credit for how things have turned out."

Was Myra being ironic? Wellesley wondered as they climbed the stone steps. Was she offering Aristocles a veiled threat, or an olive branch? The other leader would have to make of it what he would. He looked up and saw one of Aristocles's aides move closer to Myra's assistants, as if allying himself with them.

Aristocles seemed confused. "We'll see," he muttered. "We'll see."

"So where do you think the mobile went, Mr. Spock?" Kirk asked.

On the viewscreen, the green and blue orb of Tyrtaeus II was visible from standard orbit. Kirk had just finished his last debriefing with Starfleet about the alien mobile. He thought of how disappointed Admiral Lopez had looked when he heard of the mobile's final flight; Commodore Karenina had shaken her head and murmured, "What a loss—how much we could have learned!" Even if Starfleet and the Federation Council had gone along with his recommendation for a prohibition against contact with the alien mobile, they might eventually have been seeking for some way to explore it and establish contact. The aliens had been right to take the action they did.

Spock had not answered his question. Kirk glanced aft. The Vulcan was sitting at his computer station, staring intently at his display screen.

"Spock?" Kirk said.

Spock looked up. "Yes, Captain. You asked where the inhabitants of the mobile were going. I believe that the mobile will seek out some obscure system, where in time a new sun-core station may be opened up as a source of energy. It will then take up an orbit in the midst of some outer system debris, and continue with its inner life."

Uhura turned in her chair toward Spock. "How sad," she said. "I agree with Doctor McCoy—it's a tragedy to have such a civilization contemplating its own navel, so to speak."

Spock looked pensive. "I believe this case differs from the Talosian model, Lieutenant. The doctor is using that model to judge the people of the mobile, but that, I think, is a mistake. As I understand it, this culture knows exactly what it wants—to remake the world—"

"I've got it!" Kirk said suddenly, remembering the poem that had eluded him, and recited:

"Ah, Love! could thou and I with Fate conspire
To grasp this sorry scheme of things entire,
    Would not we shatter it to bits—and then
Remould it nearer to the Heart's Desire!"

"They have the energies of suns to shape their way of life," Spock continued. "But, as we learned, out of necessity—in order to preserve what they have made for themselves—they must be a culture that is shy of contact with others. Despite their isolation, they did not seem about to fall into decadence and decay and risk destroying themselves, as have the Talosians. But they can be destroyed—by others impinging on the inward world they have created. Fortunately, that has been prevented."

"What do you think, Mister Spock?" Sulu asked as he turned in his seat. "Is their way of life better than ours?"

"We will never know their achievement," Spock replied, "so it is difficult to judge. But on final balance, I am inclined to reject their way."

"Perhaps you're simply prejudiced in favor of what you think of as the real universe," Kirk said.

"Yes, because I am joined to it, because it is real, endless, and a challenge that will never be met equally, only in part."

Kirk folded his arms. "And that doesn't disappoint you?"

"No, Captain, it does not. The journey will never end, in all the lifetimes of all the intelligent life in the universe. Even the people of the mobile may one day turn outward again, with all the resources gained from their inner sabbatical. Consider: the strength of suns has only two great uses—to reshape solar systems and power the survival of intelligent life, and to shape an inner life of creative venturings. In that sense, mind and the universe are one."

"To seek and not to yield," Kirk said, knowing that he was not quite recalling still another poem. "To follow knowledge like a sinking star . . . good work if you can get it, if you have the right job."

Spock lifted a brow. "Yes, if one can create for oneself such a destiny. It is possible that we may have encountered the species that may one day seek to remake the cosmos."

"What do you mean?" Kirk asked.

"They may endeavor to destroy the cosmos as we know it, and recast the character of physical law."

"As the poet longed for?" Kirk asked.

"As they long for."

"Is that possible?"

"In a finite universe, perhaps. In an infinite one, never. But if ours is a finite universe, then the far future may see the struggle of various surviving intelligences for what to make of our universe."

"The rest of us may have something to say about that make-over," Sulu said.

Spock shrugged. "Us? There may be no 'us' after billions of years of development. We may be, what is left of us, allied with the universe-shapers."

"Mr. Spock," Uhura said, "I think you regret the mobile's leaving very much."

"It is indeed a loss," Spock said. "I strongly

intended to present them with a few questions, assuming they would have allowed me to pose them."

The four officers on the bridge fell silent. Most of the *Enterprise* personnel, except for a skeleton crew, had beamed down to the surface of Tyrtaeus II. Aristocles Marcelli and Myra Coles had granted permission for a wilderness shore leave for the crew, well away from their world's settled areas. The open regions of the main continent had much scenic beauty to offer, and the pleasant Tyrtaean climate almost guaranteed an enjoyable outing. Myra had admitted, with a rueful smile, that the *Enterprise* crew might prefer such a shore leave to one in populated regions, since Tyrtaean cities and towns offered so few amusements. But it was also politically advisable for the personnel of the *Enterprise* to keep their distance, and allow any Tyrtaeans who wanted more contact to seek them out.

"Perhaps you can show me one of your favorite trails when I beam down," Kirk had said to the image of Myra on the viewscreen in his quarters.

"I don't know if I can get out of Callinus," she had replied. "A lot of administrative work piled up while I was gone, and if I don't catch up on it now—I'm sorry." She had looked slightly regretful, but maybe he had imagined that. Maybe she was only trying to let him down easily, using her work as an excuse not to spend more time with him. There was also her position to consider. Too much obvious friendliness toward a starship captain might not be advisable.

"We were very fortunate that you were sent here on your mission," Myra had continued. "Otherwise, we could never have been sure that we were safe from the inhabitants of the mobile. Even Aristocles has admitted that much. We would have seen it enter the sun, and then leave, and we would always have been wondering—why it was there, how it could have survived the fires of a sun, what its intentions toward us were."

"Has that realization eased some of the anti-Federation feeling?" Kirk asked.

"I think it will, James. I don't know if it will aid me during the next election, but at least now I have a chance to win." She looked down, and he noticed then that she had a garment in one hand, a needle and thread in the other. "And now we Tyrtaeans must turn inward again, and go on with our lives until, perhaps, the Federation has need of whatever we have made of ourselves." Myra sighed. "Back to work! Farewell, James." She had looked regretful again before her image vanished; he had stared at the empty screen while brooding on his own regrets.

"Captain," Uhura said at last, "Request permission to—"

Kirk stood up. "Of course, Lieutenant. Permission granted for shore leave. You, too, Mister Sulu." He paused, knowing what he wanted to do. "I think I'll join you. Yeoman Barrows and Doctor

McCoy mentioned earlier that some of the crew were going to picnic near Callinus before setting off on their hike through the foothills—maybe I'll see how they're getting on."

He followed the other two officers toward the turbolift, then looked back. "Spock? Ensign Tekak-witha should be here to relieve you in two hours. There's no reason for you to stay aboard after that."

"I am content to remain here, Captain."

Kirk cleared his throat and was about to speak, then turned to enter the lift.

Alone on the bridge, Spock finished storing his records, then shut down his computer and sat still. He contemplated again the encounter with the mobile, and how it had not turned out to be the meeting with a high alien culture that he longed for. There was such a culture in the galaxy some-where, he suspected, one that was older than all the others.

What was it doing behind the scenery of stars, where newer cultures were striving for survival and knowledge? Sampling, observing, nurturing? Per-haps it was preventing great tragedies. He would probably never find it, or even any evidence that it existed. It might be best in the end to fail at this quest, he realized, setting aside his disappoint-ment—intellectual on his Vulcan side, more emo-tional from his human inheritance.

The turbolift door opened and Cathe Tekakwitha came onto the bridge, followed by Wellesley Warren. Spock rose to his feet.

"Commander Spock," Ensign Tekakwitha said, "the captain gave permission for Wellesley to come aboard. He wanted to see more of the ship's operations, so I volunteered to be his guide while I'm on duty."

"In return, I promised Cathe I'd take her back-packing in the Euniss Mountains during her shore leave," the young man said.

"I thought we'd begin at the library-computer station first," Tekakwitha murmured.

"Of course, Ensign." Spock stepped aside to allow them access; then he moved to the lower level of the bridge, halting near the captain's chair.

He looked at the planet that waited below, and he listened to the ship that would soon take him and his shipmates elsewhere. And suddenly he realized what the function of the passages in the alien mobile had been. They had not been made for physical beings to use. Those passages were wave guides for mental energies, a help in shaping virtual realities, which were then stored in panels and walls like the one he had entered.

Magnificent, he thought. They were brave and clever, the people of the alien mobile, to make inner worlds in their own image, where inevitably they would confront their deepest selves.

And perhaps he was still standing there, alive inside the perfect recreation of this, his previous existence?

He dismissed the thought. If the illusion was perfect, if it *could* be perfect, then there would be no difference. The two realities, as Earth's great philosophers Descartes and Leibnitz would have eagerly pointed out, would be one and the same. If there was even one small difference between seeming indiscernibles, the illusion collapsed. By its very nature, the infinite character of the cosmos would be forever incomplete, impossible to enumerate.

And he was content to have it so, he told himself, as an insistent beep sounded.

"Tekakwitha here," he heard the ensign say behind him. "Mr. Spock, it's the captain—for you."

Spock pressed a panel at the navigator's station. "Spock here."

"Spock," Kirk's voice said, "Myra Coles and I are inviting you to a picnic. It's a beautiful day here. Can we count on you?"

"If I may decline, Captain. An afternoon of meditation would do more to restore me than shore leave."

There was a moment of silence. "He's not coming, James?" Myra Coles asked. "But why not?"

After a moment, he heard the captain say to her, "It's his way." Another moment of silence passed. "Have a good rest, Spock."

"Thank you, Captain. Spock out."

He started for the turbolift, then glanced back. Ensign Tekakwitha and Wellesley Warren were at the library-computer station, sitting much closer to each other than strictly necessary.

"Ensign," he said, "the bridge is in your hands. I will be in my quarters if you need me."

"Aye, sir."

In his quarters, Spock sought sleep, meditating as he drifted on how closely sleep resembled death, and how much he disliked even the idea of nonbeing. It was, for him, the greatest evil, especially when imposed by deliberate violence, cancelling all thought, knowing, and appreciation.

Earlier today he had said, "The Tyrtaeans have their dream, and so do the Tyrtaean rebels. The Federation has its dreams and ideals. The people of the mobile have their dream. . . ."

"What are you getting at?" Kirk had asked.

"Just this, Captain. All these dreams have one thing in common, with different means for achieving them, of course. And that is that unwished-for realities keep breaking into their dreams—"

"Yes," Kirk had said, "but each has responded to and dealt with its intruder, and perhaps been changed by the encounter." The captain had been silent for a few moments, but then had asked, "Spock, on balance, what do you think of the Tyrtaeans? There seems to be much satisfaction in their stoic ways."

"Yes," Spock had replied. "Stoicism, as a philosophy, harbors the illusion that self-control and worldly influence may be treated as one and the same. It is in some ways an admirably practical way, but it fails in the extremes."

"As do most things," Kirk had said.

Spock had nodded. There was more to say, of course, much more. . . .

He thought for a while of what that would have to be, and how he would phrase it. Then he remembered the second piece of poetry, lines from Tennyson's *Ulysses,* that the captain had somewhat mangled:

To follow knowledge like a sinking star,
Beyond the utmost bound of human thought . . .
To strive, to seek, to find, and not to yield.

And when he was finally asleep, Spock dreamed that he was awake and at his post.

About the Authors

Pamela Sargent and George Zebrowski have been watching *Star Trek* ever since the 1960s, when they were students at the State University of New York at Binghamton.

Pamela Sargent sold her first published story during her senior year in college, and has been a writer ever since. She has won a Nebula Award, a Locus Award, and been a finalist for the Hugo Award; her work has been translated into eleven languages. Her novels include *The Sudden Star, The Golden Space,* and *The Alien Upstairs.* Her epic novel *Venus of Dreams* was listed as one of the one hundred best science fiction novels by *Library Journal. Earthseed,* her first novel for young adults, was chosen as a 1983 Best Book by the American Library Association. Her other acclaimed science fiction novels include *The Shore of Women* and *Venus of Shadows;* the *Washington Post Book World* has called her "one of the genre's best writers."

Sargent is also the author of *Ruler of the Sky,* a historical novel about Genghis Khan. Gary Jennings, bestselling author of the historical novel *Aztec,* said about *Ruler of the Sky:* "This formidably researched and exquisitely written novel is surely destined to be known hereafter as *the* definitive history of the life and times and conquests of Genghis, mightiest of Khans." Elizabeth Marshall Thomas, author of *Reindeer Moon* and *The Hidden Life of Dogs*, commented: "The book is fascinating from cover to cover and does admirable justice to a man who might very well be called history's single most important and compelling character."

Sargent has edited *Women of Wonder, The Classic Years* and *Women of Wonder, The Contemporary Years*, two anthologies of science fiction by women. With artist Ron Miller, she collaborated on the forthcoming *Firebrands: The Heroines of Science Fiction*. Two new novels, *American Khan* and *Child of Venus*, are works in progress under contract to HarperCollins.

George Zebrowski's twenty-six books include novels, short fiction collections, anthologies, and a forthcoming book of essays. His short stories have been nominated for the Nebula Award and the Theodore Sturgeon Memorial Award. Noted science fiction writer Greg Bear calls him "one of those rare speculators who bases his dreams on science as well as inspiration," and the late Terry Carr, one of the most influential science fiction editors of recent years, described him as "an authority in the SF field."

Zebrowski has published more than seventy-five works of short fiction and nearly a hundred articles and essays, including reviews for *The Washington Post Book World* and articles on science for *Omni* magazine. One of his best-known novels is *Macrolife*, selected by *Library Journal* as one of the one hundred best novels of science fiction; Arthur C. Clarke described *Macrolife* as "a worthy successor to Olaf Stapledon's *Star Maker.* It's been years since I was so impressed. One of the few books I intend to read again." He is also the author of *The Omega Point Trilogy,* and his novel *Stranger Suns* was a *New York Times* Notable Book of the Year for 1991.

Zebrowski's recent novel, written in collaboration with scientist/author Charles Pellegrino, is *The Killing Star,* which the *New York Times Book Review* called "a novel of such conceptual ferocity and scientific plausibility that it amounts to a reinvention of that old Wellsian staple: Invading Monsters From Outer Space." *Booklist* commented: "Pellegrino and Zebrowski are working territory not too far removed from Arthur C. Clarke's, and anywhere Clarke is popular, this book should be, too."

Zebrowski's *The Sunspacers Trilogy* was published in 1996 by White Wolf/Borealis Books. He is editing an original anthology series, *Synergy,* for White Wolf, and working on two novels, *Brute Orbits* and *Cave of Stars,* for HarperCollins.

Pamela Sargent and George Zebrowski are also the authors of *A Fury Scorned,* a *Star Trek: The Next Generation* novel. They live in upstate New York.

Coming Next Month from Pocket Books

#46

TO STORM HEAVEN

by

Esther Friesner

Please turn the page for a preview of

To Storm Heaven . . .

Geordi La Forge became aware that he was not alone. The sensors in his visor that served him in lieu of eyesight touched off an uneasy feeling that he was being watched. He looked all around, but there was no one there. The corridor he had chosen to explore was empty, though there were several doors lining it, as well as many pillared alcoves made to display an assortment of Ne'elatian art treasures.

He considered knocking on one of the closed doors, in case anyone was in who could help him on his way, but Blumberg's words echoed in his ears and he stopped short. It was one thing to ask directions of a Ne'elatian encountered in the hallway, quite another to go hunting up a native guide. Geordi couldn't have explained the difference if anyone had asked him, but he knew at gut level that doing the latter was tantamount to surrendering something very precious to him. A Starfleet officer was resourceful—took a healthy pride in being resourceful—but a Starfleet officer who was blind knew that resourcefulness was another word for independence, and independence was the most precious thing he owned.

As he stood there in the hallway, a cool breeze brought him the scent of alien flowers. Cautiously, he followed his nose. *Maybe I can find the gardens without asking directions after all,* he mused as the scent grew more distinct. *I should have thought of this before I lost Yee and Blumberg. It's getting stronger. We must've been closer to the gardens than we thought.* The flowery perfume led him on until it reached him at a sharp angle, from a doorway to his left. Now it was so intense that he was sure that he was on the threshold of the palace gardens. He turned and went through, expecting to feel the sun on his face and to hear the sounds of the musicians tuning their instruments for the promised concert, an event specially staged to honor the visiting Starfleet crew.

Instead he felt the same cool, perfumed breeze and saw neither gardens nor musicians nor fellow crewmembers, but the startled face of a young Ne'elatian woman. She wore a plain green robe, and her hair was hidden by a veil of the same color, its gauzy material held in place by silver netting. She was very lovely.

Geordi smiled. "Excuse me, but could you please tell me how to get to the palace gar—?"

She dropped to the floor before him, face pressed to the cold stone, arms extended and crossed above her head. "Let there be mercy for this one, unworthy as I am to hear your words, starlord," she said. She sounded as if she were on the verge of tears or panic or both.

Geordi's smile was gone. He squatted down on his haunches and looked at the woman closely. "I'm sorry, I didn't mean to scare you. I'm just lost. I want to find the palace gardens. Could you please—?"

She moaned and wrapped her arms over her head, as if cowering in anticipation of a blow. "Starlord, forgive me for having displeased you in this or in any desire you might have." The words were muffled, but Geordi still managed to hear all she had to say. "My spirit is still imprisoned by the flesh; its flaws have led me astray. My glorious teachers warned us that we would do best to keep to our rooms while you deigned to walk with them in the undying light of Evramur. I disobeyed. I heard there was to be music, and there is no sweeter sound than the celestial songs of Evramur. My greedy spirit thought it would do no harm to go secretly to hear it. I should have known that there is no thing that can be kept secret from the glorious ones. My sins are many. I admit them freely and give myself up to any penance necessary, even though it might be exile from the joys of Evramur." Her slender shoulders shook ever so slightly as she began to cry.

Geordi stayed where he was, staring at her, completely at a loss. At last he reached out his hand and touched her gently. "Don't cry," he said. "Please."

She lifted her face, copiously streaked with tears, and asked, "Is this—is this your will, starlord?"

"Yes. And also that you stop calling me starlord." He stood up, giving her a hand to help her rise with him. "My name is Geordi La Forge. What's yours?"

The irises of her brilliant turquoise eyes dilated with a mix of consternation and fear. Then she ducked her head and said, "I must go." She jerked her hand from Geordi's grasp and ran away.

He never knew what possessed him to race after her, he only knew that he couldn't let her escape him. Her robes were long and voluminous, hardly the best thing to wear for efficient running. He caught up with her easily. As soon as his hand fell on her shoulder, she hit the ground again, alternately imploring mercy of the starlord and declaring her unworthiness to receive it.

Geordi leaned back against a pillar and slid down it until he was seated cross-legged beside her. Very patiently he said, "I think there's been a mistake. I told you, I'm not a starlord, whatever that is. I'm Geordi La Forge, chief engineer of the U.S.S. *Enterprise*. You don't have to tell me your name if you don't want to. I'm sorry, maybe I was out of place asking that. I don't know the customs here on Ne'elat. I'm here on shore leave, just visiting your planet, and there's supposed to be a concert taking place in the palace gardens. I'd like to hear it. Would it be all right for you to take me there?" He felt odd, talking to the back of the young woman's head, but she was so tightly curled up into a protective ball that it didn't look as if he would ever get to see her face again.

Pity, he thought. *It's a very beautiful face.* He settled his shoulders more comfortably against the pillar, ready to wait as long as it took for a reply.

His patience was rewarded. After a time, the young woman tilted her head sideways and looked up at him out of the corner of one eye. He tried his luck at luring her back into the open with another smile. This time she raised her head and slowly uncurled her body until she was seated on her heels, facing him with a look no longer fearful, but merely uncertain.

"Ne'elat?" she asked. "Why do you call this place Ne'elat?"

Her question took him aback. He'd never had to explain the name of a planet to one of its own inhabitants, especially not when he knew that it was the same name the inhabitants had given that planet in the first place.

Maybe she thinks I'm talking about the palace itself, he reasoned. *They might have an official name for it, like the House Adorning Peace on Canis II or the Talking Lodge on Lamech V. She probably thinks I've confused the name of the government palace with the name of her planet.*

"I'm not calling this *building* Ne'elat; I'm talking about this whole world," he said. He accompanied his words with an expansive gesture, and hoped he had set things straight between them.

"World?" She shrank into herself as she echoed the word, panic edging back into her voice. "How great is your realm, starlord, if you can call boundless Evramur no more than a world?"

Now it was his turn to be bewildered. "What are you talking about? Evramur? I've heard you use that name a couple of times already. What's Evramur?"

She bowed her head reverently and folded her hands on her bosom in much the same dove-shaped sign that Meeran Okosa had used when he recited the saga of lost Ashkaar. "Holy Evramur, blessed Evramur, realm of untold sanctification, Evramur who shows herself robed in beauty on the evening horizon, Evramur from whose mouth the breath of life bathes us, her unworthy children. Here in her bosom our spirits never hunger, here our lips never thirst, here we find rest from all labor and know the peace that all pilgrims seek."

"You make it sound like . . . paradise," Geordi

said, and when she shyly asked the meaning of that alien word, he explained it for her as best he could.

When he was done, she smiled. "But that is Evramur, your paradise: refuge and rest of the deserving spirits who have left the flesh, haven to those less worthy, whose flesh still anchors the spirit, such as I."

"You——?" Geordi wasn't exactly sure of whether or not he wanted to ask the next question. He was a little afraid of the answer he might get. This young woman was as charming as she was beautiful. Unfortunately, charm and beauty were no guarantee of sanity. No, there was no help for it——he gained nothing by willful ignorance. He had to ask. He had to know. "You think you're there? In Evramur? You believe you're . . . dead?"

Her laughter brightened his world. "Starlord, you are gracious. You condescend to tease me. Have I not said that the flesh still holds me? Of course I am not dead!" She spread her fingers and held them like a latticework between them, then said, "But I hope to be. Is it for that you have come, great starlord? To take me from the shell of flesh that weighs me down? To free me at last from tears and sleep and breath?" Her hands fell to her knees, revealing a face transformed with holy ecstacy. "Oh, yes, it is so! It must be so! Starlord, take what you have come to take freely, with all my will! Tears, sleep, breath!"

She threw herself forward into Geordi's arms and locked her mouth to his in an impassioned kiss.

Look for STAR TREK Fiction from Pocket Books

Star Trek®: The Original Series

Star Trek: The Next Generation®

Star Trek: Deep Space Nine®

Star Trek: Voyager®

Star Trek®: New Frontier

Star Trek®: Day of Honor